SAVAGE CREATURES

NATALIE WILKINSON

First published 2016

Original illustrations by Megan Claiborne

Big Bang Press
bigbangpress.com
Twitter @BB_Press

Formatting by BookCoverCafe.com

ISBN
978-0-9904844-6-2 (pbk)
978-0-9904844-7-9 (epub)
978-0-9904844-8-6 (kindle)

Brooklyn, NY

1. Fiction. 2. Fantasy—Fiction. 3. London–Fiction. 4. Family–Fiction.

2015951879

Jamie is fairly certain she'll have about half an hour before someone tips off Jack. She hasn't been back to The Stag in a while, so if she's lucky, she won't get kicked out too soon. It doesn't help that her shitty glamours never hold on neutral ground, so it's a chore to keep her face out of sight well enough to settle in the darkest corner. She'd really rather not have to face Jack today. It would be some kind of miracle if this client showed up on time, though, so she's trying to prepare herself for the worst-case scenario.

She would just as soon have met elsewhere, but he'd insisted. The Stag is an old, old meeting place for their kind, and what the client wants, the client gets.

It's probably a generalization to say that tourists are a pain, but in her experience, they tend to be lackadaisical, confused, and impossibly prone to blocking exits on the tube. As such, Jamie is really not expecting the man who enters the bar a few minutes before their agreed-upon hour, looking deeply put-out by the rain he's shaking out of his thick, black hair. *You ought to know better*, Jamie wants to tell him. *Wear a hat.*

There should probably be some doubt in her mind that this is the client, even though she hasn't seen him before, just heard his voice over the phone, but shifters aren't thick on the ground in cities, and he's not hiding it very well. The shape of his face is slightly off: his pale, glassy irises are slightly too big for his face, and reflect the wall-mounted lamps before he blinks furiously, re-adjusting for the lack of gloom. She's heard it happens to some of them; that those who spend a good deal of time on four legs or in the air can never quite remember what they're meant to look like, after. Jamie likes to think that if she were capable of becoming an animal at will, she'd take a photograph of herself as a reference for changing back. But what does she know? She's only got the one body, such as it is. Her abilities lie elsewhere.

The sluggish crowd is necessary if not pleasant, their rumbling mixture of voices all blending together. The mass of bodies hides Jamie well enough for the time being, a melting pot of everyone Jack has been slowly cultivating over her many, many years of running the place. The exact date of the establishment is impossible to pin down, but it seems to have been long before anyone Jamie knows was born.

The old-timers are interspersed with a few stragglers who've somehow gotten the address, standing at the bar or hunched over corner tables like she is: other weirdos that the rest of London would just as soon shuffle under the rug. Some of them, she thinks wryly, even look normal. Maybe if you didn't know what you were looking for, you wouldn't be able to tell, or maybe this is part of Jamie's own particular weirdness. The ability to look at people and just *know*. Sarit—who is, after all, normal—had always tutted when she'd put it that way (*weirdness, freak*) but Jamie has never been especially bothered by difference. She already has her fair share, after all.

If Sarit knew she was here, she would probably have a heart attack. It's good, Jamie figures, to have somebody looking out for her who actually has her head screwed on straight.

The man spots Jamie almost right away, which is worrying. Doubly so, as it happens about the same time the bartender, Alfie, does, the glass she's rubbing perfunctorily with a greasy rag hitting the bar with a decisive thump. The icy look she shoots Jamie's way is unmistakable.

The timing could be better, but skipping out now and risking a terrible first impression is definitely preferable to staying and making a scene with Jack and Alfie in front of the client. This is what she gets for being stupid enough to agree to meet somewhere she's officially been banned for life, she guesses. Well, nothing for it now.

Jamie has never been sure Alfie is entirely human, but has never been able to confirm that she *isn't*. The lack of precise knowledge she has of what Alfie could feasibly do to her has always left her a bit unsettled, so she'd rather not chance it. So Jamie just winks at her, grabs her coat, and jumps out of the booth, shouldering through the evening crush. The din makes a helpful cover for Alfie's shout as Jamie grabs the shifter by the wrist, grins her most charming grin, and says, "Can't fault you for the time, but let's find a quieter spot, yeah?" hoping confusion and surprise will converge into a moment that will let her carry them outside unobserved.

The man yanks his arm out of Jamie's grip. "You're Jamie?"

"Beggars can't be choosers," Jamie says, spotting Alfie's intimidating bulk heaving her way towards them. "I'm off with or without you, so think fast."

"What?" His thick, straight eyebrows draw down in beautifully obvious confusion. It's really quite interesting, the way his expressions lag. Jamie has no real facility for disguise, unfortunately, though she can pull together a passable mask in a pinch. She would love to learn how to do that, how to commit that performance to memory. It might be to her advantage one day, to be able to seem like a different strain of freak than she really is. Shame there isn't time enough to get a detailed store of visual references now.

"I'm going to run now," she says, enunciating clearly, just in case there's some kind of accent issue at play here, before taking off, weaving through the smokers outside taking shelter from the downpour and bursting out into the chilly October rain.

The usual tingle in her fingers is a full-blown, burning itch by the time she makes it over the neutral threshold, magic crackling as she passes back into the regular unbounded roar of London. Despite her formidable power, Jack can't hold anyone on neutral ground, so the pain is an inconvenience rather than a crippling deterrent. Maybe she isn't quite as angry as Jamie thinks she is. That's a useful piece of information, or at least it might be.

She's finally had enough of sprinting about a hundred meters out, bursting out of the alley onto the high street and slowing to a brisk walk to catch her breath, hoping to be thoroughly ignored by the crowd of pedestrians trundling angrily along under their umbrellas. Jamie's about to chalk the evening up as a bust when the client grabs her by the shoulder.

Jamie smacks his hand off and turns around. "Wouldn't do that if I were you."

His hair is flattened against his high forehead, rain dripping slowly into his eyes. "You're not. Is this how you usually meet your clients?"

It takes all the self-control Jamie possesses not to laugh at how similar the effect is to watching a cat slowly succumb to a shower. "I'd buy a hat if you're planning on staying in London long," she tells him, biting her tongue to stop herself from commenting further, fully aware of the fact that she's now almost as wet as he is, the hem of her trousers beginning to drip into her shoes.

"I'm not," is the only the response she gets before the man is brushing past her, shoulders broader in the fading daylight than they had seemed in the dim pub, arm stretching out to hail a cab. It's an uncomfortable minute or so, since it's the tail end of rush hour and taxis are few and far between, especially when people are trying not to ruin their clothes and choosing to hand over the fare instead of waiting for the bus.

"I'd say we'd better call this a failed partnership and go our separate ways," Jamie says eventually, when it becomes apparent that the man won't be swayed by persistent failure. She shoots a distrustful look at the black cab that finally pulls up to the curb.

"Get in," the shifter says shortly, before leaning in the window and speaking quietly to the driver. Jamie catches the address and cringes. It's nowhere near her territory: far too full of people with aggressively disciplined workout schedules and children named Tarquin.

"Are you getting in or not?"

Jamie yanks her attention back to the cab, where the door is open and the interior is dry, and figures that at the very least, if she's about to get murdered, it probably won't be worse than what Jack wants to do to her. Someone sent this poor bastard her way for a reason, anyway, and Jamie just made him sprint in the rain; there's probably some kind of balance to be restored. "Yeah, all right. You're paying."

"Fine." At the very least, the man's American accent is unusually enjoyable, if Jamie's being honest, and that's only a fifty-fifty bet at the best of times.

She climbs in, settling herself on one of the folding seats, water sneaking under her collar in an unpleasant trickle as the cab starts to move, driver eyeing her in the rear-view mirror. Jamie reaches around to turn off the intercom, taking in the way the shifter is sitting perfectly upright, arms crossed over his chest. He's not quite visibly nervous, but there's something brittle and guarded about him, something that suggests he might not like the close quarters in which they've found themselves any more than he liked the noise of a crowd. Jamie can work with that.

"So. I understand you're looking for someone."

"I hope that's not a surprise."

Jamie snorts. "You'd never have been sent my way otherwise. It's what I do."

"She won't want to be found."

"Well, we'll fucking see, won't we?" Jamie grins, aiming for conspiratorial.

They sit in silence for a long moment before the man holds out his hand. "Francis." His palm is warm, and would probably be dry if they hadn't both just come in off the street in a rainstorm. It's a good handshake, firm and well trained. He releases her thin, spidery grip with careful blankness, just a beat too late.

"So, if we're going south we'll be in here for a while. I dunno where you're from, but we've got traffic down to a fine art here." As if to punctuate the statement, the taxi lurches to a halt at a pedestrian light, then stays there as the little red numbers of the meter tick higher.

When another long minute passes without Francis saying anything, she sighs. "Who is it?"

He blinks.

"The person you're looking for," she clarifies, speaking very slowly, as though he might not be able to understand what she's saying.

"My sister," he says after another moment's pause. "Can't I just—give you something of hers, and you can…" He makes a vague gesture and she tries not to laugh. Shifters, she's been led to understand, tend to live in seclusion: the last big tribe she knows of in Britain is off in Wales somewhere. Maybe nobody ever taught him anything useful.

"In a manner of speaking," she says. "It generally helps to have some information first."

He shifts uncomfortably in his seat, water still dripping down his face. "She… vanished," he says carefully. "A couple of months ago. We've been looking for her."

"Like, kidnapped vanished?" she asks. "How do you know she's here?"

"She left me a voicemail," he says, irritated, although she's not quite sure whether it's her he's irritated with, or his sister.

"Really."

"Saying—saying she was here," he says. "So, we decided I should come."

"*We* decided?"

"The family," he says blankly, as though this is a self-evident fact.

"All right," she says. "And she didn't just, I don't know, answer her mobile when you called her up? Assuming you did, in fact, call—"

"No," he says, scowling. "And she's gone from the apartment where she was staying."

"We say flat here," she tells him, grinning with all her teeth. "Well, fine. I can't say I completely understand what exactly you're all playing at, but I'm not above taking your money, and finding her shouldn't be too much of a problem."

He sighs and sags back against his seat, visibly relieved. The cab has been inching forward in the traffic, rain sluicing down the windows; it'll be ages until they arrive. Francis keeps twitching minutely at honking horns and the squealing of brakes, the kind of fine tremors that only someone watching very closely would pick up on. Jamie knows stress, but she also knows London, and is largely unfazed by its endless cacophony of sound and its atrocious weather and the way it always smells like wet pavement even when the sun is out. Francis is so obviously a visitor here, and doesn't seem particularly suited to the chaos of a city. Now that she looks more closely, she can see that fine, almost imperceptible lines keep appearing and disappearing at the corners of his eyes.

"How did you get my number, anyway?" Jamie asks, to kill time.

Francis frowns. "The woman who owns the bar," he says. "I think her name is Jack?"

Jamie stares at him for a moment. "Really."

"Should I not have?" he asks.

"No," she says, although now she's suspicious. Jack hasn't passed any business along to her in over a year. Sleeping with her, Jamie thinks sourly, had had its benefits, even if Jack herself had reaped most of the advantages from Jamie's work.

She looks at Francis appraisingly as his face shifts just enough for her to notice. This could all be some kind of elaborate set-up. But no—if Jack really wanted to come after her, she'd do it herself. Besides, Jamie's been lying low recently, for better or worse. Her wallet could be considered an expert witness on that one.

"So, how does it work?" he asks. He's looking at her as though he's trying to drill holes in her head with his eyes.

She wonders how rude it would be to remind him to blink every so often; the combination of very pale irises and very dark hair makes him look like he's been drawn in broad brushstrokes, a lazy artist's rendition of a human face. Maybe he's stressed and it's showing, his body fighting to keep its form.

She taps her fingers against her leg. "Well," she said. "It's really not so complicated. You give me some of her blood, if you've got it—doesn't have to be much—and I do my work, and then I tell you where she is and you go track her down."

He stares. "What?"

"Well, what did you think?" she asks. "I'd use a crystal ball? This kind of thing needs a link, you know?"

Francis doesn't react, except to narrow his eyes and fold his arms across his chest, lean muscle corded tight under his changeable skin.

Nonplussed, Jamie runs a hand over her own hair, trying to feel out how it's drying. There's no helping the way it sticks up regardless, the wild, tight curl of it irrepressible unless she shaves it right down.

"What did you plan on giving me?" she asks. "I can't get by on just an old shirt, I'm not a miracle worker. We can use your blood if need be. A sample from a close relative can do the job, up to a point. It can even work better, sometimes. Fresher."

Francis stares and Jamie pauses, watching his face. Most people who come her way are desperate enough to try anything, even if that means skirting close to darker practices. There are all kinds of cranks on the streets of London, peddling all kinds of magic that simply don't do anything, from love potions to cures for cancer to—yes—spells for finding lost loved ones. And there are people who can point a client in a general direction: *Try Manchester. Try Glasgow.* But there aren't many people at all who can do what Jamie can do: *She's coming out of Victoria Station. He's in some woman's flat in South Croydon and I don't think you want to know what he's doing. Do you want some distinguishing landmarks?* She's not unfamiliar with clients who are uncomfortable with something as taboo as blood work, but she also knows that desperate people are willing to compromise a surprising number of firmly held beliefs if it means getting results.

She makes a quick decision and reaches out, laying a hand gently on Francis' forearm, just to see what he'll do. "It helps if you're thinking about who you're looking for, but you can just try to keep your mind blank, if that works better for you."

Francis doesn't say anything for long enough that Jamie thinks she's lost him, and has resigned herself to walking home in the rain, but finally he breaks the silence.

"You're not a psychic," he says, voice flat enough that Jamie can see he's rethinking the decisions that led him to this point, which is about what Jamie expects from most people, whether they're entirely human or not. It dawns on her that there's a serious disconnect in their assumptions about what was going to happen here today. She wonders what Jack was playing at—in Jamie's experience, people don't react well to being faced with surprise blood work. It doesn't matter that the more benign practices often don't work: people don't find them nearly as unsettling.

Jamie pulls her hand back from him, scooting further back to her side of the seat. "I never claimed to be anything I'm not," she says carefully.

"No, you didn't," he agrees, and Jamie relaxes marginally.

"Did Jack tell you I'm a psychic?"

"No—I just told her I was looking for someone. She didn't mention that you're a—that blood would be involved."

Jamie decides not to wonder what he was going to call her—leech and vampire are both traditional and unimaginative, and she can't imagine him saying "soul sucker." Bloodhound would be more technically accurate as well as poetic, although the *bitch* connotations are less than appealing.

In the hierarchy of their little universe, she ranks near the bottom of the social totem pole, but she has never wasted time wishing she possessed some more publicly acceptable form of magic. She is what she is and she can do what she can do, and if other people don't like it, that's fine by her. She'd rather have more than her fair share of ability than be popular. And she isn't hurting anyone—not now, at least, she thinks bitterly.

She hasn't always been so morally sterling, but there's no use in belaboring old points. She's got a routine, and though it would be gauche to admit it, the rush she gets when she works is... difficult to obtain elsewhere.

Unfortunately, being a social pariah does sometimes make it difficult to do business without a patron, and she's been on her own for some time now. Since that was her own damn fault she supposes she just has to tough it out until business picks up.

She suppresses a sigh, and focuses on trying to salvage the situation. She could really use his money.

"Well, this is what I do," she says slowly. "I use blood to find people. And if someone sent you my way, you've got blood, or very nearly, and you wouldn't have come this far if you had anything else to go on."

Francis' face remains frozen in a frown of consternation, and Jamie can't tell if he's simply indecisive or if his failure to keep his face shifted has somehow resulted in his expression being stuck that way. She wants to laugh, but even in her head the joke sounds more manic than it did before, when they were out in the rain. If he doesn't make a decision— or make a move—then she's prepared to cut her losses and ditch the taxi, her mental map prepared with quick and tricky exits highlighted in red. Her fingers are curling behind her back on the door handle when he finally responds, sounding excessively polite: "I don't think I'll be needing your services. I'm sorry about the misunderstanding. I can have the taxi drop you off somewhere else."

The patter of rain outside has lessened. The taxi still hasn't made much progress, scooting along in stops and starts. "Well, don't toss out my number just yet," she says. "I might not be psychic, but you might need it again before this is all over." She slips out the door and, because she isn't above having the last word, throws out, "Make it quick—say by the end of the day?—and I'll even throw in a discount and comp the consulting fee."

Shame. It seemed like a big job. She's desperate enough that with another potential client, she might have pushed harder, but he'd seemed brittle enough as it was. Still, better safe than sorry, and he clearly needed some time to come to terms with the idea. She can't deny that a part of her is relieved. He was probably going to be more trouble than he was worth.

London has a history of fires, but she'd rather not jump into the flames just yet.

Once the taxi drops him off and he's over the threshold of the dingy basement apartment where he's staying, Francis slumps against the wall, releasing his hold on the little alterations he's been trying to keep in place for hours. A long sigh shudders out of him almost involuntarily.

He rubs absently at the skin of his forearm, trying to erase the sensation of warm, thin fingertips, goosebumps coming up again at the memory. He knows it's a necessity, hiding his face, but there's an odd disconnect in trying to talk to someone through somebody else's features, all while trying to block out the noise and the smell and the itch of discomfort prompted by strangers. It's a relief to finally let his body slide back into its natural planes, to lose some of the bulk and heavy, burdensome flesh he's wrapped himself in.

His phone vibrates, hot and angry against his leg. He's been ignoring it lately. He knows exactly who's calling, and he doesn't want to speak to her. His shoulders hunch at the thought.

He wasn't entirely honest with the woman—Jamie—when he said they'd decided he should come after Catherine. It was their mother who had called him into her sanctuary, which still always made him feel like a child about to be upbraided for doing something wrong, and told him that he was going to go to London and find his sister and bring her back, and that if he didn't get it done fast, she'd come after him herself. Francis hadn't wanted to leave home—he'd never been out of the deep woods, the mountains; never been anywhere with so many people or so much concrete. But he'd also never said no to his mother about anything, and Catherine was her favorite child. Catherine was the heir. Without Catherine... without Catherine, well... She had to come back, simple as that.

The string of texts will be terse, the voicemails worse. He pulls out the phone and systematically deletes his messages, rubbing at his face with a sigh. London is chaotic, anxiety prickling along the back of his neck, but he's found himself oddly fascinated by the streets curving away from the eye in patterns devoid of logic; the riotous, disordered architecture; the river snaking through it all with a total lack of concern, serpentine and deceptively slow-moving; even the people—all the many, many people, more than he can comprehend could live in such a small space. He can't honestly say that he *likes* it, but he can at least admit that he's intrigued—and he's rarely intrigued by much.

Francis can't help but admire Catherine's determination, even if he has none of the same drive. She has proven maddeningly difficult to find. At least he knows that she hasn't been murdered—or at least, the message says she hasn't. He thinks he'd know, but it's different without the faint certainty he's never tried to explain.

"You know what twins are like," his aunts and uncles used to joke about the two of them. As far back as he can remember, he and Catherine have always seemed to know where each other are, what they're doing, what they're feeling—at least, until now. Now she's just a haze, a blur—a shape in the distance.

He's listened to that voicemail a dozen times. He's probably started to hear it in his sleep. The heavy breathing at the beginning, which he somehow knew was Catherine's even before she spoke. And then: *Bet you weren't expecting to hear from me. I'm not dead, in case you were worried. You were, weren't you? I bet you were just terrified... What would happen to you if I died? I'm not sure. Would you just—vanish? I wonder... I wonder... You know, I thought about asking you to come with me. I did. But then I thought—he won't say yes to me. You know that's true. I'm in London, by the way. Little walk down Dad's memory lane. You could come looking for me, if you want. Maybe we could have a heart to heart.* She'd burst out laughing. *Tell Mom I don't want it, by the way. I'm saying no. Bye, Francis. Sorry to make you the messenger.*

Their mother hadn't reacted at all when he'd played it for her, just sent him away, and then called him back two days later. "Well, I can't go," she'd told him brusquely. "So you had better."

Would you just—vanish? He can't work any of it out. But then, for all their closeness, Catherine has always been something of a mystery to him. Catherine was bright, glittering, eloquent; he hated to talk. He liked to shift around in his changeable skins: that was what he had always been good at. Catherine had never had that same ability. She'd never been strong, not like he was; she always resented him for the ease with which he slipped in and out of bodies, flitted joyfully between them before he really knew that it wasn't so perfectly, beautifully simple for everybody. So she was jealous: he had always known that. But so was he. So *is* he, he corrects himself. She isn't dead. She isn't *really* gone.

"Who the hell fucks around with blood for—" Francis starts, speaking mostly to the ceiling. He shakes his head out as he walks over to the couch, stewing as he thinks about the woman's thin, brown face, her riot of tight curls, her laughing black eyes. All of it coalesces into a sharp, jagged picture of someone amused and hardened, reaching across the backseat of the cab like she had the right to—to *touch*, demanding the kind of link that takes decades to earn, in Francis' family. *Blood*. So she had blood magic—fine. His family does, too, and they have for centuries. It's just a different, wilder kind than whatever this woman knows. She didn't have any idea what she was getting into.

He had been right to decline, probably. Nobody would fault him for failing to pursue that avenue, considering the risks—and yet a part of him wanted to say yes. He almost had—had almost pulled out his claws and sliced, just to see what would happen. The part of him that knows what it feels like to have the taste of it on his tongue had wanted to see another person take it, learn it, make it—no.

His phone sits, inert, on the table. If he leaves it off, maybe he'll sleep better. The lie sounds weak even in his own mind: he won't. He'll jerk awake at every noise, wondering if he's protected himself well enough to deserve rest; wondering whether his soft, vulnerable innards are too exposed like this, long and hairless and utterly devoid of any natural defenses. Maybe he could chance a shift, choose a form and curl up on the couch as something predatory. It's tempting, alone in a new city, but lately, shifting takes longer than it should. He's been trying not to think about it—he's just tired. It'll pass. It sometimes feels like his whole body is creaking, like his joints are breaking when he changes. Maybe, he thinks, it's the damp English air. Maybe it's London. There's too much noise here to risk it, anyway. The street sounds, the ever-present rumble of cars, would all send him deeper than he's comfortable thinking about, and there would be nothing familiar to reliably pull him back out.

He runs through places Catherine might have gone by rote, as he has countless times every day since he arrived, forcing himself to concentrate on the task, just in case he's missed something obvious, something anyone with half a brain would have seen. But he doesn't think he has: he's been here more than two weeks already and he hasn't had any luck. If he had, he wouldn't even have bothered with a psychic, let alone someone who deals in blood.

His phone breaks the near-silence like a church bell, clanging loudly enough to set his teeth on edge, his own heartbeat suddenly thunderous in his ears.

He hurries to pick it up, scrabbling at the table, too on edge to even check the number. Few enough people would have it.

"Hello?" His own voice sounds strange to him, rough, far away.

"So you did follow me?" Catherine sounds amused, her detached voice holding the same careful tone she used to use when they were kids, when she told him stories he always, always believed, no matter how outlandish they were, how fundamentally implausible. They were twins but he had always felt like the younger of the two of them, the more naïve.

His breath comes shallowly as he listens to hers on the other end of the line. He can almost imagine her smile, the way her lips always tug up on the left side first. "I bet you hate it here," she says.

"Where are you?" He swallows, unsure why his palms are sweating. "Catherine, you can't just—"

"Always the messenger, Francis." She laughs, harsh and low in her throat. "I'm not coming home."

There are so many things he should say, now that he has her on the phone: he should threaten her, cajole, use the words he fought so hard to learn, all the things their mother tried to teach him before she tired of his single-mindedness when all he ever wanted to do was sink down and *hunt*.

You have to, he could say. *Without you, it all goes to shit. You're the only heir. The only one who can do it.* The only girl who ran around with the rest of them growing up, the sacred child, kept cloistered in their mother's room so many long afternoons, safe from harm, leaving Francis defenseless against all the older boys. Even if clan leadership couldn't only pass to girls, she would have been the obvious choice: she wasn't as gifted a shifter as Francis but she was so much smarter than he was. There was a certain light around her.

"Why?" he asks instead, wondering what she could possibly say to try and convince him to stop chasing her. She has to know that it's not really up to him, that the last thing he wants is to be the one forced to stand between her and the rest of the family.

"Isn't it enough that I don't want to?" She sounds amused, like she's in on a joke he doesn't understand. If she were here he'd try—no, if she were here they'd fight. They'd probably rip at each other until they were bleeding, until even she lost her grip on speech and just tore at him. It happened so rarely when they were kids, her losing control of her temper, but he still remembers the sick satisfaction of it, of watching her crack and knowing that he'd done it. Knowing that he'd made her bring out her claws.

"You know it isn't." He's not sure why it hurts to say it,

when it's only the truth. "You know you can't just leave."

"I knew you'd say that." She pauses, breathing heavily, static following in the wash of air. There's a heavy, silent moment as their breath syncs up, both exhaling in tandem, as though she's standing next to him, passing judgment. "I can't change anymore."

Francis' hand clenches down on his phone so hard it starts to creak. "Yes you can, it doesn't—it doesn't just go away like that." What she's saying is impossible for him to contemplate, something huge and overwhelming. She's trying to create fissures in a lifetime's solid bedrock of conviction. It doesn't *go away.*

"Is it harder to come back, Fran?"

"No," he lies. His grip on the phone feels precarious, as though his hands are slowly disconnecting from his body, mouth suddenly dry at the thought that she just might be telling the truth.

"Really."

"No," he says again, and then, a moment later, almost against his will, "it's just—it's just being in a foreign country—"

She lets out a low, mordant laugh. "I don't think so, Francis. I think it was probably the exact day I decided I didn't need to put up with her trying to *mold* me anymore."

He doesn't say anything. It's not possible, what she's

saying—it *can't* be possible. But—he can remember the day she left. He was so sluggish he almost couldn't get up. That was only one day, but then—ever since—

"You're wrong," he says gruffly.

Catherine goes silent for such a long time that he thinks she's hung up the phone, but the low hum of the connection holds him still, keeps him breathing. If he rushes her, she *will* hang up, and he can't let her go just yet, can't hang up without knowing what she knows, without finding out how she can possibly tell him something he hasn't yet admitted to anyone at all.

"You've never wanted to be anything other than what you are, have you?" she asks.

Francis doesn't know what to say. What he *is* is mutable, by definition. His body is change, no matter how many times he comes back to the same form. It used to be easy to relax, to settle back into the broad, dexterous hands and the satisfying height of his human shape, and so easy to know that he'd never been trapped in it the way most people are, that the potential refuge of claws and fangs was never far away. The easy fluidity of his body, furred or smooth, barbed or benign, has always been a kind of blessing, even if the uses he sometimes puts it to have lately made it seem more like a curse, late at night, when he's alone with his thoughts.

"Why should I?" he asks, wondering what he'd be if he

weren't this, weren't something so attuned to change that the thought of being chained to one body is enough to freeze him in his tracks.

"You'll see soon enough," she says after a while, voice low, static still whispering between them, and doesn't explain further. A moment later, in a more straightforward tone, she adds, "You don't have the right to drag me home, Francis."

"I don't have a choice," he forces out.

Catherine laughs, short and sharp, and he can imagine the way her head tips back, throat vulnerable and unprotected. "Everybody has a choice." She doesn't wait for him to answer, probably because she knows what he would say. She hangs up on his inhale, leaving him ready to argue with the dial tone, panic fluttering in his gut.

Jamie flops down on Sarit's sunken brown couch, sure she's going to have to keep looking for work.

Sarit sighs, shutting her computer with a snap. "You *had* to lead with the blood?"

"It's easiest if people know what they're getting into," Jamie mutters. "'Sides, I actually grabbed him while Alfie was chasing me out the door, so no, I didn't lead with it, technically."

"Small mercies." Sarit says wryly, sitting back in her

work chair and pushing her glasses up into her bleached hair, sending it flying out to the sides like a brittle halo. "So what happened?"

Jamie thinks about how to explain it—the shapeshifter, the meeting at The Stag—and just doesn't have the energy. She throws her arm over her eyes at the idea of having to do this over again: having to keep dodging around Jack if she wants anywhere safe to meet clients, or being forced to take risks elsewhere. It all seems like too much effort.

Sarit's expectant pause turns awkward before she sighs, huffing through her nose. She gets up, heavy boots thudding on the uneven floorboards until Jamie knows she's standing next to her, heat and faint jasmine smell and funny blurred outline looming over Jamie's prone form. Jamie tenses, expecting the questioning poke to her sternum she probably deserves. Instead, she gets a small, short-fingered hand in her hair, pulling gently through the damp, coarse mop. She's going to shave it, soon as she can be bothered.

"You're going to have to do something about Jack, you know." Sarit keeps petting her, shoving her sideways with one amply curved hip before perching next to her, speaking down to Jamie's covered face.

"Or I could avoid Jack forever. She did *ban* me, after all. Chucked me right out."

"I'm just saying, if she ever decides to exact revenge upon you, she knows where to find you. Besides, she did have her reasons."

Jamie snaps out of her incipient relaxation, alarmed. "Suppose I know who got you in the divorce, then."

Jamie's under no illusions as to what she'd do without Sarit. Starve probably, at minimum. She's known Sarit long enough to have thought they were inextricable, but then, one of them is a wall and the other a climbing vine; it's not necessarily a symbiotic relationship. In any case, the prospect of having to strike out without her is—daunting, to say the least. She's had Sarit to rely on, in one way or another, since she was seventeen and out of control—even younger and stupider than she is now. Sarit's been as young but Jamie doesn't think she was ever stupid, not like everybody else is at that age.

A tremor starting in the very tips of her fingers tells her she'd better get her heart rate under control or the night will end on an even lower note.

"Not hardly," Sarit says mildly, poking Jamie viciously in the side as soon as she relaxes. "I only ever knew her because of you. I'm just not an idiot. Besides, I'm normal. Someone has to watch out for you, after all."

"Yeah, thanks for that." Jamie sits up, uncovering her eyes, blinking back her sight as she kicks off her shoes. She curls her knees into her chest, resting her chin on folded arms, breathing deeply. "I'm—"

"Done with her, I know." Sarit sinks further into the couch cross-legged, hands cradled in her lap. She's heard the story a hundred times by now, and still listens. "I'm not saying give her one last farewell fuck," Sarit continues. "Maybe—"

"A quickie in the taproom and a tip towards the debt?"

Sarit laughs, a high little bark that tends to startle small children and nervous animals. She shoves at Jamie, shoulders tensing, pushing her out of her nervous fold, prompting her to sprawl as Sarit arranges herself with most of her torso in Jamie's lap. "Well, you ballsed it up, so you can't run forever if you want to stay in town." She stares up at her, small, heart-shaped face faintly childlike from this angle. "So, are you going to fix my neck or not, I've been writing up this fucking file all day."

"Bored housewife?"

"Bored house-husband, actually." Sarit rolls her eyes. "Makes a change."

Jamie settles a palm under the back of her head, the other slipping around the tense muscle at the base of the neck before she twists, feeling the rippling crack of released tension.

"Serves you right for having a proper job," Jamie mutters, tugging gently at her hair.

"Part time," she corrects, without much venom. "Not all of us have what you've got, some of us are just freak-adjacent. Have to make due on brains."

"What makes you think having a talent makes me an idiot?"

"The part that shoots itself in the foot all the time," she says sharply, elbowing her as she gestures widely. "The part that can't dump someone without leaving loose ends." Sarit sighs again, shifting against Jamie's legs until she's more comfortable, draping herself, catlike, over the stretch of her thighs. "Well," she says at last, "could be worse, yeah?"

"Yeah," Jamie agrees, wondering how close she can cut the lie before Sarit sees it on her face. Jamie's never been the one to do the dumping.

"Cheer up, then," Sarit orders.

Jamie lets her head fall against the back of the couch, staring at the cracks in the ceiling. "How much do I owe you now?"

"Best not to think about it, it'll turn you gray." She puts her glasses back on. "Look at it this way, at least you've got no student debt."

"I can pay you in sexual favors."

"Ha. Best to save that for people who haven't already sampled the goods."

Jamie winces, grimacing up at the crack that's beginning to look a bit like a basset hound: droopy, inbred, and bemused.

"Leave it, please." Jamie would rather not admit how tempting the idea of selling things other than her skills is right now. She's never particularly minded, truthfully, and although she and Sarit have never really seen eye to eye with her on this particular issue, she'd only put up a cursory fuss. Nobody sneers at money, no matter where it comes from, unless they have enough already to be choosy.

Sarit closes her eyes for a second, taking a deep breath before she nods.

Jamie pulls out her phone, hoping the pre-payments will last a while longer, and nearly falls off the couch. "Well, fuck," Jamie says.

Sarit laughs, leaning forward to see. "Hey," she says, "looks like you've got a client after all. Does this mean I'm getting rent?"

Jamie just grins at her before she bolts out the door, declining to answer.

☞

An odd tugging sensation is what drags him to the door. He could call it paranoia, a certainty that his hideout here is going to be overrun at any moment, and it wouldn't be untrue, but the thing that really does it is the irrational certainty that Jamie will be outside. He doesn't have any view of the street, but he presses his ear to the door, wishing he could risk giving himself better hearing without being useless afterwards, body taking just incrementally longer to recover each time. It's the foreign air, he thinks stubbornly, mulishly. That's all it is. Catherine's just fucking with him like she always has. She's just winding him up.

All he hears is the ambient noise of a quiet street in a busy neighborhood: distant sirens, the sounds of people so far away that they become part of the scene. He opens the door and sure enough, Jamie is there waiting.

Francis watches her smoke. She's leaning against the low wall outside the flat, apparently in no hurry to finish her cigarette. Francis is glad she's at least willing to be here, but is less impressed with the way she sticks out, with her worn boots and wild hair, disheveled and sleepy-eyed. He tries not to glare as she takes a last, long drag and lets all the smoke in her lungs out through her nose, draconic.

A blonde woman walking her dog and yapping on a phone about some kind of cleanse makes a face and crosses the street to avoid her, eyeing Jamie suspiciously from the opposite side of the road until she disappears round the corner.

Francis wonders whether she can tell: whether it bleeds off of them somehow, what they are and what they have inside of them. He's never spent enough time around the rest of the world to know. His mother and all his older relatives—aunts and uncles once and twice removed, the unbearable posse of boy cousins who used to make his life hell as a kid, an endless litany of relations that he couldn't remember not knowing—had always told him that people hated them out there. They dealt with their own kind. But in London Francis has had the funniest sensation of being a non-entity: it's as though everyone's eyes just slide right over him, and everyone else like him; as though even The Stag isn't quite real. As though they're all walking through streets nobody else can see, or maybe doesn't want to. He doesn't know if that can exactly be called hatred: it seems more like purposeful indifference. But maybe those amount to the same thing.

"That was fast," he says, in lieu of anything more relevant, and Jamie stubs the butt of the cigarette out on the heel of her boot.

She gestures with what remains of her cigarette, the sweep of her wrist taking in the state of her clothes, intermittently splattered with dry mud and the dust of old buildings. "I know the roads."

"Are you finished?" he asks, and she raises an eyebrow at him, hands shoved in the pockets of her coat, smoke dissipating slowly, fading into the watery daylight.

"What does it look like?" she replies, voice flat, full lips thinning.

He isn't sure whether he's accidentally insulted her or not, but that's not his problem. "Come inside," he says, wanting to get this over with as quickly as possible.

"Sure." She rocks back on her heels, looking expectant, and it takes him a second to process that she's waiting to be led somewhere. He turns his back, trying to breathe the tension out of his shoulders. If she were planning to take advantage of being out of his direct line of sight, she probably would have managed to already. Besides, he might not be entirely sure about the breadth of her abilities, but he knows his own intimately, knows how best to rip into a body for easiest access to the vital organs, knows which arteries bleed out fastest. He takes no joy in it, but defending a territory isn't clean work. And if there's anything his family has trained him to do, it's that. Their kind lives by a different set of rules. He may not be used to roads, and trains, and crowds, all the ephemera of regular human life—but he is used to violence.

It's easier in his rented apartment, somehow, to hold a face. The lack of noise allows him to settle more easily, to adjust his features until they're just off from his own—close enough to maintain, but distinct enough that Jamie won't be able to accurately identify him later. An uncomfortably insistent part of him wants to just drop it, but that's not wise.

The door clicks shut behind Jamie, and the silence that descends between them feels heavy, expectant. Francis isn't sure how to break it. Some wild, irrational part of him wants to tell her that he has his own reasons for wanting to find Catherine: that he only called her back after pacing around the apartment for hours after hearing that all-too-familiar voice on the phone, and then trying to forget it.

Catherine may be fucking with him but he can't ignore her. He never has been able to, never in the entire course of their lives; they've been burrs in each other's sides for as long as he can remember. There was a time, when he was younger, when he would have been thrilled for her to vanish, to leave him alone, even if it meant leaving him to deal with the nasty pack of cousins he could never escape; with Uncle Gordon, who had always disliked him especially, for reasons he couldn't quite grasp; with his *mother*—at least, that was what he thought then. He and Catherine were a united front against outsiders but they could hurt each other better than anybody else ever could and sometimes he thought there was nobody else he wanted more badly to escape. Now he thinks he knows better. He thinks maybe that as crazy as they make each other that they aren't supposed to be apart—thinks maybe they aren't supposed to be away from home at all. There's a reason for the order of things and he isn't going to be the one to break it. He can't let her, either. He thinks maybe if he could just find her and go home that everything would go back to the way it used to be, has always been. Go back to being right.

"This place is a tip," Jamie says, incredulous, eyebrows rising as she kicks an old box out of the hall. "Not exactly what I was expecting." She grins at him, looking vicious with delight in the murk.

Francis looks around, taking in the uninhabited sprawl of the basement. It was the best he could get his hands on without drawing too much attention to himself: quiet neighborhood, nothing outside to indicate that somebody who shouldn't be there was coming in and out. For all he knows, Catherine's been watching him the entire time he's been here. It seems more than plausible.

"It's got what I need," he says. In this case, a rickety table and chairs, grimy with neglect, and a bed, not too badly off with dust.

Francis feels himself start to slip, reaches up to rub at his eyes, hopefully quickly enough to mask it. *Damn.* He's still fighting to get his control back when Jamie's fingers land very, very lightly on his forearm. Francis jerks his arm away, tamping down on a snarl. "Don't." He's not willing to let her feel anything she can't already see.

"You don't have to do that, you know." Jamie takes her hand back, squinting shamelessly at him, long eyes narrowing noticeably. "I know that's not actually your face, and at this point I can mostly promise you I'm not going to do anything to hurt you deliberately." Her grin doesn't diminish. "Besides, what would I mug you for?"

"You can *mostly* promise?"

"No guarantees."

She smirks. Her teeth are surprisingly even. Francis has no idea why he'd thought they'd be crooked, aside from her generally off-kilter demeanor. Maybe it was the sinking suspicion that she's been punched in the face at least once, or the way her smile falls just slightly on the wrong side of mean. "I'd rather see what your results are like than hear any more promises."

"Touchy," Jamie mutters. "Shall we?"

She shoulders past Francis and heads toward the kitchen, hands shoved into the cavernous pockets of her army-green coat. Francis follows her at a careful distance, wanting to keep her in sight. Jamie carelessly kicks a chair out and flops down into it, sprawling out with her legs splayed, jeans ripped open near the knees to show bony joints.

Francis sits cautiously in the chair next to her, turning to face her. "So, how do we do this?" His skin is prickling at the thought of giving up any vital part of himself, but he's brought her here for a reason. He's already made up his mind. He thinks of Catherine on the phone. *Is it harder to come back, Fran?* He doesn't really think he has a choice.

Jamie eyes him appraisingly, crossing her arms over her chest, jacket loose at the shoulders. Francis finds himself rethinking his impression of her. She's still thin, dark skinned, long-limbed and taller than her slouch suggests. Francis thinks now that maybe she has the bones of someone who should be heavier; she certainly has the eyes of someone older than her apparent twenty-odd years. She's lean in the way runners are lean, but now he wonders if that's by choice.

"Well," she says, "first you pay me."

"Right," he mutters, flushing, and fumbles for his wallet in his pocket. He never had to carry a wallet at home: there were a lot of things he never had to do. He counts out the money and hands it over to her. He has the distinct impression that she's trying not to laugh at him.

"Not a haggler, I see," she says, raising an eyebrow, and the money vanishes into one of her many pockets. "Well then." She cracks her knuckles, an anticipatory expression crossing her face. "I'd rather take it straight, but—"

"No." He won't—no, that won't work. He doesn't want to leave the taste of his skin on anyone's lips.

"Yeah, I didn't think you'd be keen." Jamie shrugs. "Glass'll do, then. Just a bit, yeah? Let's not go overboard."

Francis gets up without a word, going back into the kitchen and reaching into an abandoned cabinet at random for something that will suit her purposes, hoping to get this over with as quickly as possible. He comes back with a little glass bowl and a small knife, sharp enough to do the job, even if it's a little rusted and he'd rather use claws. Better not to. "Now?"

Jamie's crooked smirk turns hard. "It's your blood. Does seem like you're in a rush, though."

Annoyed, Francis takes a deep breath, exhaling his frustration by blowing dust out of the bowl, and makes a cut just deep enough on the back of his wrist for blood to flow freely for a few seconds, dripping across his fingers and into the bowl. The bright, deep red is mesmerizing against the clear glass. They both watch as the stream tapers off, blood obeying its biology and closing the wound. He stares at the dark pool in the little glass bowl, but doesn't slide it across the table toward her just yet.

"How does it work?" he asks, without looking up at her.

She lets out a little huff. "Pretty sure I already told you that," she says. "You give me the blood, I find your sister, I get paid, you get a heartwarming family reunion, everybody wins—"

"No," he interrupts, "I mean—how do you do it."

"Ah," she says, and pauses. "Well, how do you think?"

There are all kinds of blood magic. Francis has no facility for magic of any kind except the obvious, the kind that resides in his cells, in his bones, but other people in his family—well, there are other people with different skill sets. Blood marks territory, blood can bind two people together for life. Blood can sometimes even raise the dead, as long as their bodies haven't been cold for too long. His mother used to talk about how it was part of their *history* and *heritage*, but it never felt like that, the few times he saw people die to make a spell possible. Death, in his experience, never feels like anything other than a particularly vicious present.

Most of it isn't like that. Jamie's, evidently, is not either. That doesn't mean he has to like it. It's fruit from the same tree. "Why don't you tell me," he says to her.

"I eat it," she says, and he twitches. He can feel his face shifting. Why, he wonders, didn't she say drink?

"What else do you think?" she asks. "Just looking at it's not gonna do a thing, I'm sorry to tell you."

"Is that all you do?" he asks, and she tilts her head. "The only kind, I mean."

She goes still for a moment. "Yes," she says finally, and he can tell that she's lying about something, though he isn't sure what. "Do you want me to do this or not?"

He drops the knife and shoves the bowl over to her. He wants this to be finished. "Here. Make it fast."

"Can't rush art," Jamie mutters, eyeing him strangely, and hooks a finger over the rim to pull it the rest of the way towards her. She glances back up at Francis, bowl held delicately in her long hands. "Last chance to say no."

He rubs his hands over his thighs, palms sweating. "Just do it." He does his best to think of Catherine—her laugh, her sharp eyes, the way she's always managed to make him feel like a fool—and waits.

She raises an eyebrow, eyes raking over his face for an instant before she tips her head back and pours the blood into her mouth. He blanches as her eyes go entirely white, color bleeding out and leaving nothing but blank space in its wake. Her body has gone rigid, her fingers slightly twisted around the bowl and pressed against the table. She doesn't seem to be breathing. He hasn't ever seen anything like this before. He expects something spectacular, maybe, to end it, to show him that it's worked, but all that winds up happening is that Jamie, wide lips stained red, swallows and gasps, collapsing face first onto the table with a groan.

Francis, alarmed, reaches over to shake her, just to make sure she isn't dying. He doesn't think it would be too difficult to lose a body in this city, but he'd rather not have to.

She smacks his hand away before he manages to touch her, shoving herself back into the chair, pinching the bridge of her nose with a grimace, teeth stained red to the gums. She blinks a few times, eyes fading back to their normal dark brown, a frown tracing a crease between her eyebrows. "No, that's—" she breaks off, shaking her head. "That can't be right."

Francis recoils, on edge. "What happened?"

Jamie licks her lips, eyes closing. "You're twins, yeah?"

Francis goes cold, feeling oddly violated by the blunt question. He nods before realizing she can't see him. "Yes."

Jamie's fingers tap the wobbly table, following no particular rhythm until they resolve into a beat. "Okay, well. I've got good news and bad news." A manic grin stretches across her face, made all the more disturbing by the pink wash of her teeth. "She's not far, but—" She closes her eyes again, head tilting back as though turning her face to the sun, the movement slow and deliberate.

Francis opens his mouth, but realizes he hasn't got anything to say. Finally, he asks, "What are you doing?"

"Pulling," Jamie replies matter-of-factly. "I know what you are, you know. You can stop hiding." She points, bitten-off fingernail aimed straight at his forehead. "You've got a slow heartbeat," she says, and then suddenly, for no reason Francis can discern, she chokes, slides off the chair, and lands unconscious on the floor.

☞

The impact takes her by surprise, crack-thud of her knees hitting stone, the sharp copper rush of blood seeping between her teeth as they dig into her lip, making her hiss. She reaches out and grabs whatever she can. When she takes her hand away it's streaked white, slightly greasy. She rubs her fingers together and then wipes them on her shirt.

It's dark down here. If she could still change she could make herself see better—even she could always manage that. She squints, trying to make out the end of the tunnel. Her legs are covered in mud.

There's no map of these places, these underground caverns. She wonders whether they would move around if somebody tried: they seem to defy order, organization, the outside world. You don't deserve to be here, *the air seems to be saying to her,* unless you've worked at it. Unless you can make your way through on your own. Even blind. Trial by fire.

She pauses, panting. She's so tired lately. Everything makes her so tired. Sometimes she just wants to lie down and sleep until she dies or Francis finds her. But it's not her that wants that, not really—it's her body. And she isn't really her body. She's discovered that lately, though maybe she always knew. Knew when she tried to push it into doing what she knew on some level it should do, and it refused to comply. Of course, she's not sure Francis could really call his body his *either. It's too many bodies crammed into one. As though he's looking for something he's never quite been able to find.*

She looks around. It feels like she's in a room. Something crackles faintly here: some kind of energy. It's not enough, but it's something. Her skin buzzes. She's closer, closer. And then—then—

What will happen? She drags her hand over her face and stops when she feels something slick. She pulls it away and looks at it. Whatever was on the walls—lime. She thinks it's lime.

She leans against the wall again, not bothering to worry about the state of her clothes. She's getting closer. And Francis—she smiles—Francis is getting closer to her—

❦

"Fuck me." Jamie jolts awake, every breath rough in her chest.

She presses her hands to the floor and tries to remember where she is. There's something bizarre thrumming in her. Something wrong. Normally this kind of magic is simple, easy: a sense, almost under her skin, of direction, place. Something dragging her along. Until she can say: *Yes. That's it. There you are.* The kick of a high, as addictive as any drug. And then she sends people on their way. But this—this—

The basement flat. The shifter. *Francis.* She feels herself smiling somebody else's smile. *He's getting closer*— Her head is killing her. That's where she is: that's his name. Francis. She can still feel Catherine's teeth in her mouth if she tries hard enough. Or if she lets herself stop thinking about it. She presses her eyes closed.

"Are you all right?" he says cautiously. She groans, and looks at him. His face swims into focus above her, his heartbeat nearly deafening. She wishes she could tell it to shut up.

Francis doesn't move to help her up, but he doesn't seem to be in a hurry to kill her, either; so on balance, things could be worse. But everything is different than it should be: there's an urgent pull to the blood under her skin, something like a deep current beneath calm water. Enough to sweep her aside for a while, at any rate. The hair on the back of her arms is standing straight up, her skin too tight, and something is thudding deep inside of her. She feels like she could crawl out of her own skin. Or like her skin isn't her own. Or maybe like her skin itself might shift at any second.

"You said—'I know what you are,'" Francis starts hesitantly. He's sitting on his heels, dust settling on his shoes as he watches her come to. "What did you mean?"

She stares up at him, uncomprehending. "What?"

"That's what you said," he says. "Before—" He gestures instead of finishing his sentence.

"No idea," Jamie tells him. "I don't remember."

"Well, what about her not being far?" he asks impatiently. "Do you remember saying *that*?"

She blinks, and thinks for a moment. "No," she says. "But you're right, she's not. Far, that is."

"*Where?*" he demands, as though every second that passes is making some vital difference.

Jamie presses her palms against her eyes and sucks air past her teeth, the taste of blood turning metallic on her tongue. "Don't you ever get rattled?" She shoves herself up on one elbow, half expecting scraped palms and a bloody chin, but her skin is just the usual map of little cracks and old scars. She shudders.

Francis looks at her, head tilting just slightly to one side, and she realizes his features have slid again, this time settling on something finer, as though the thicker lines he'd been holding onto earlier were just a gradient alteration. He looks younger, too, eyes still wide and pale, but with a thinner sweep of an eyebrow, an even sharper contrast between skin and hair.

Francis frowns, ruining the effect. "Not really."

"Well that's fucking inhuman," Jamie mutters, staggering to her feet. Standing up, she feels even more clearly the heartbeat thumping in her skull that isn't hers, and isn't Francis' either. She shakes her head to clear it, without success. "She's underground. She's looking for something. I don't know exactly why." She braces herself on the table until it starts to creak dangerously, willing her nausea to subside.

Francis' heart speeds up, just enough to throw her off again. Jamie wants to head back to Sarit's flat and sleep for a thousand years, but she hasn't done her job yet. She might not have a lot of pride, but what little she does is tied to having enough of a reputation to maintain a steady stream of work. "Come on."

"What?" Francis reaches out to steady her and makes contact before she can skitter away. "That wasn't part of the deal."

Jamie wrenches her arm out of his grip. "No, don't—" She takes a deep breath, closes her eyes despite the new wave of dizziness, and concentrates, following the living threads in her mind: one spooling out towards Francis, red and dark, only active enough to beat with his heart, and the other, fraying in the distance, but strong, vividly crimson, twisting downwards and out of sight. Still, it doesn't feel like Catherine is far away. If anything, it feels like she's in the room with them. Jamie's skin is crawling.

She swallows thickly, opening her eyes for balance if nothing else. "Listen, this isn't what I'd normally do, but—" She gestures, at a loss. "You want to find her fast and I can't—normally I'd be able to tell you exactly where she is, but this time I can't, and you'll just have to trust me. I can find her. I can take you to her."

Even to her own ears, it sounds like a lie, as though she's pulling some kind of scam, but it's the truth. She braces for an outburst anyway. Everyone has a limit, and she must have reached his by now.

Francis is standing too close to her, staring at her face but not making eye contact. Jamie squares her shoulders, unwilling to show any more weakness.

"All right," he says. "Lead the way."

Jamie exhales slowly. "What?"

"Lead the way," Francis repeats. "If you waste my time I might kill you."

"You're a freak," Jamie tells him, room finally beginning to level out except for the throb of heartbeats lapping in her ears and the red thread, ghostly in the corner of her eye.

Francis steps back, looking at the door. "Maybe," he says, voice quiet. "It's hard to tell."

Well. Jamie can't really argue with that. She makes for the door, thinking that she was right about at least one thing. Family pulls tight.

Jamie follows the thread until they hit the riverfront. The orange lamps wash the other colors out of everything in sight, even Francis' pale skin taking on a sickly russet glow. She ambles her way along the rest of the bank at a fairly sedate pace, unusually knackered. The aftertaste of blood still hasn't quite left her mouth, acrid and metallic under the welcome flavor of smoke.

It's been a long time since she was back here. This area is pretty far off her usual turf, but if she remembers it right, the cracked-concrete grayness gives way about a mile from here, boat slip next to an old church sloping innocuously down into river mud, littered with old shoes. She glances over the railing, facing into the wind, to check the tide. Not as low as she'd like, but close enough.

"Can you swim?" she asks Francis, to make sure she's not leading him somewhere he can't go.

The pull of the blood hasn't faded yet, settling heavily in the back of her skull. The weight of Catherine's distant life is setting her just off-balance, a low hum of frantic, uncertain energy, especially this close. She practically feels like she could touch her.

Catherine, for all that she's been running, wants to be found: that much Jamie could tell, from the electric buzz of anticipation when she thought of her brother coming, the certainty of her knowledge that he *would* come. She's playing some kind of strange, deliberate game, and Jamie doesn't know the rules— maybe Francis does, but she doesn't think so. He seems lost, adrift in the hustle and bustle of the city, baffled by his sister deviating from whatever the hell their usual norm may be. Jamie figures it probably doesn't typically involve picking up and heading to foreign countries without a trace. She could tell him, of course—she thinks she could maybe explain a lot to him, but she can't help but think it might be wiser to stay quiet. She has a gut instinct that this kind of urgency is out of character for him, and it's always useful to hold something back for later.

At least Jamie got a better look at his face this time, all hard bones and wide-set eyes, straight mouth pulled tight at the corners. Francis hadn't even noticed himself doing it, probably, the slide back into what has to be his real face—if he even really has one. The shift was so slow that Jamie had only caught it because she was already looking.

In the distance, Catherine moves, sending a prickle of cold sweat down the back of Jamie's neck. It'll fade. It always does.

She lights another cigarette as they round the corner past the massive block of glass-and-chrome flats shining dully on the riverfront, stepping into the little churchyard, stone squelching under their boots. Jamie puts a new cigarette between her teeth, looks at Francis to make sure he's behind her, and hops the railing.

The first few meters of the plunge are always the worst, mud rushing up to meet her as though greedy, ready to seep into her clothes and eyes and mouth, contaminated and treacherous. Instead, Jamie lands on the stairs and quickly makes her way along the concrete siding into the church's jagged shadow, breathing a reflexive sigh of relief around her mercifully dry cigarette.

Francis lands beside her with a splash, mud going all the way up to his knees, his greater weight sending him in deeper. "Where are we going?" he asks at last, wiping flecks off his palms onto his ruined trousers. "If you're trying—"

"There are roads," Jamie says quickly, trying to smoke as fast as possible before they go down into the damp. "Faster ways to get around, but fast isn't always best. Stick close. The other routes aren't pretty."

Francis grabs the cigarette out of her mouth and flings it away. They both watch it land in the mud beside the abandoned hulk of an ancient houseboat, half-sunk into the bank. "Is this going to get me to Catherine faster?"

Jamie snarls at him and then hisses in pain, pressing a hand to her temple as the blood pulses. "Fuck. Yes, all right? I want this out of my head as much as you want your crazy sister."

Francis frowns, expression lagging. "She's not crazy."

Jamie's headache still hasn't faded so she doesn't bother trying to argue. Instead she just picks her way across the tidal sludge. The grate is where she remembers it, thankfully, chained over and half-buried in silt. She has to wade a few meters to get there, but at least the mud is only ankle deep at the moment.

She rattles the grate, waiting impatiently as a brief stir of movement flickers in the darkness behind it, chain falling away, slithering back into the tunnel as the grate swings inwards.

Inside is marginally drier, and there's someone sitting in the gloom a few feet down the tunnel. A loftier person might describe this individual as a gatekeeper, but in truth they look more like a weedy kind of nightclub bouncer, sitting on a stack of car tires with their face hunched over a glowing smartphone screen: all told, a disgruntled and vaguely female-looking shape with a downturned mouth.

"Hair or nails?" asks the gatekeeper in a bored tone, eyes flicking up and down Jamie's mud-spattered outfit. A small pair of scissors flashes into view, offered up in one long, slightly misshapen hand.

Jamie looks back at Francis to gauge his reaction before taking the scissors and snipping off a quick slice of thumbnail. It isn't like her body parts are a hot commodity, anyway. Her skills work the other way around. Hopefully no one down here will notice that Francis is a shifter. Hopefully she and Francis won't bump into anyone at all.

She drops the fragment of nail into a proffered container, their journey now bought and paid for. Francis looks intrigued, if the raise of his eyebrows is anything to go by, but he doesn't protest. Probably he's just glad to avoid handing over any of his own offcuts to strangers in the dark.

"How far can we get with this?" Jamie asks the gatekeeper, hoping it will be enough that they won't have to surface somewhere too crowded.

"Tide's coming up," she says. "You might make Tower. Isle of Dogs or Limehouse if you're lucky."

It's not ideal, but it could be worse, if not for the massive headache that's settling in deep behind her eyes, flashes of pain alight with phantom sounds, accents, and the peculiar cadence of another heartbeat. "We'll take it."

"Ha. Thought you'd be a harder sell."

"Caught me on a good day," she mutters, brushing past her into the low, dank tunnel. The light fades, but unlike Catherine, who came untried and untested on somebody else's information, Jamie doesn't really need light to navigate down here. She's spent enough time that she could close her eyes and make her way through the maze unscathed. It's all about instinct—and besides, she has the thread of Catherine's mind to follow.

"Stay sharp!" She calls back over her shoulder, feeling rather than seeing Francis close behind her, watching her own muddy boots make the first set of tracks this pathway has had in quite a while. People get nervous, under the plague pits. She doesn't care so much, personally. It's not exactly pleasant, but then, nothing in London ever is. You're always standing over dead bodies in this city, one way or another.

Personally, she's more concerned about the fresh ones. Nothing that's properly dead has much in the way of a wish to do harm. It's the stuff that's not all the way gone that's the trouble.

Jamie inhales, settles herself on Catherine's heartbeat, and closes her eyes, following the pull of blood through living veins.

Francis swipes at the condensation on his face, fighting to breathe past the miasma of mud and what he hopes isn't raw sewage in the shallow water. He's not dressed for this, unlike Jamie, who seems utterly unconcerned with the dirt, one hand trailing along the ancient bricks, fingers leaving dark streaks where the pale lime is scraped away by her nails.

He takes the opportunity to watch her, squinting through the darkness. She's focused, rarely pausing when they come to junctions, turning left more often than right but never once seeming to falter. Her shoulders seem bony even through the coat. There's dried dirt on her dark skin and knuckles. In profile, she has a long nose, bridge just slightly domed as though it's been broken at least once.

Francis wonders if he was a fool to trust her. Her main motivation is, at least, reassuringly prosaic: money. And if she were trying to trick him, she'd probably make an effort to be less unpleasant. Still, he's getting a new understanding of the desperation that leads people to do new and dangerous things. These mud-filled tunnels, for example, are an unexpected development.

He takes a deep breath, feeling the catch of his ribs, his discomfort down here, enclosed on all sides and not willing to risk anything more than blinking a few time to sharpen his eyes, for fear he might—well. He looks around as they walk. What does Catherine need down here? There's something off about the air in these tunnels, something that he can almost taste, but he can't quite place it, almost as though it's a language he doesn't speak. It seems unfathomable to him that she would come all the way across the ocean to go running around underground in some dirty tunnels. But that is, apparently, exactly what she's chosen to do.

Ahead of him, Jamie stiffens. "Try not to get worked up," she says, looking back over her shoulder. "Just try to take calming breaths or something. I'm working here, and you're—" She makes an odd gesture, hand jerking between them. "Interfering."

He snarls, breath still tight and high in his chest. "How do I know you're not just—"

"Fucking with you?" she smiles, not at all friendly, and he's reminded of red teeth and white eyes. "You don't. But I'm not."

He's about to say something, words unplanned, just borne of frustration and claustrophobia, but she freezes, eyes wide in the gloom, before darting closer and clapping a dirty hand over his mouth. Purely on instinct, he bites her.

He breaks the skin and then recoils, lips tinged with chalky residue from her palm and the acrid taste of human blood.

Jamie flinches and grimaces, but doesn't let go, fingers cold as they dig into his face. She doesn't make a sound. Startled by his own reaction, Francis starts to push her away, but despite her size, she's solid, immovable.

"Shut up," she grates out, voice barely audible, before she grabs him by the sleeve, heedless of her punctured palm, and starts to sprint down the last fork, no sound but the trickle of water and the drag of breath to give any sign of what she's running towards—or away from.

Francis digs his heels in, jerking his arm out of her grip, fighting to pull his teeth back before he speaks. He's about to demand an explanation when a faint echo reaches them, acoustics disorienting, seemingly coming from above.

Jamie points, and Francis looks up. A rusted-over grate is set in the arch of the tunnel, nearly obscured by years of corrosion and the grime of neglect, but light filters through, enough to make Francis blink, discombobulated, as he approaches.

Jamie's eyes, meanwhile, have gone white again.

"Is she—" Francis' mouth feels coated, tongue thick and not quite back to the right shape.

Jamie pinches him, managing somehow to find a spot where his shirt gapes to find skin, tethering him with her nails digging into the faint pulse beneath the tendon in his neck.

Francis abruptly feels flush with heat, alien to the damp of the crumbling brick tunnel, sweat breaking out across his shoulders and dripping down his spine. He doesn't pull away, too aware of the rush of blood in his ears, the sudden absence of cold a shocking reminder of how long it's been since he felt warm.

"Listen," Jamie whispers, "they're in the crypt."

Francis doesn't hear anything at first, too occupied by the scurrying of nearby rats, their whiskers a slightly different shape from the ones at home, their tails shorter and more prone to being misshapen. They're moving away from the direction Jamie is facing, startled away from something. But then: shuffling footsteps. Heavy breathing. Low murmurs.

Something like dread slides down his spine.

Jamie looks at him when he doesn't reply, then pinches the bridge of her nose, fingers leaving messy streaks of lime across her face. "I have to ask," she mutters, "is there a reason you're desperate enough to use me to find your sister, because I think there are some—she keeps fading in and out, and she's been moving fast since we got here, but now—"

Francis has a moment of hesitation, unsure how much of what he's feeling is just paranoia over being so far off course that he had to employ a stranger to come into family business. He just can't predict how all this will play out, or whether he's ahead of or behind the curve. Past experiences would suggest that he won't be able to count on his own luck.

"I thought I was the only one looking for her," he says. It's true, although he was never sure how long that would last after he arrived in London. He wasn't exactly expecting his mother to bring the whole family. Besides, this can't possibly be her—he'd be able to tell. The footfalls are wrong, and all the other sounds. The weight of it. Francis doesn't know who these people are.

Jamie nods, though not necessarily in agreement. She looks like she's made up her mind about something. "Could always be other people passing through."

"What are the odds?"

Jamie looks at him. "Low."

Jamie can't help the draw: there's something disruptive about crypts, the settled-in death of hundreds of people seeped into the dirt and bricks built up around and under them, London's grisly legacy concentrated in what she can only feel as thrumming pulses of magic under her skin, part of the vast body she occupies. There's more power in these stones than anywhere else in the city, if you know how to use it. Most people would never even think to look, and then would be horrified if they did: the idea of drawing on all those bones is unpalatable at best. But Jamie isn't especially concerned with societal mores. She's always felt at home here, ever since she happened upon the old paths as a truant child, long before she'd discovered what she was. Something in them had called to her.

The only problem is that she can't walk into one without losing focus, the brimming hum of so many dead, even hundreds of years after the fact, diffusing her until she feels eerily becalmed, just a ship in the doldrums. Everything starts to feel less than urgent in the presence of all those lives folded into each other and the ground. She shakes her head to snap herself out of it.

They're good places to hide, these crypts. After she first discovered them, she used to come back more than was strictly healthy, often between being shuttled around from aunt to uncle to ever more distant relatives, none of whom wanted to put up with her for more than a few months at a time. She was not exactly an easy child.

The more potent crypts have long been barred off, but some were just sitting there, open to the passing masses. Most people were oblivious to what sang out beneath their feet, which Jamie had always felt was holding her close, and which others experienced as cold fingers creeping down their spines. She really should have realized she was a freak earlier, she thinks now, but it's not like you get a card in the mail. That would make things a lot easier.

It would be impossible to know and catalog every ancient death beneath the streets, but places where blood pooled and settled, places where life was thin and fragile and not taken for granted—those pull in a way she only realized was unusual years after she had set out on her own. Jack had sent her on the path of discovery, had explained certain things to her, but she suspects she would have reached the same destination eventually either way.

She hasn't been down here so much lately. The magic she's been doing doesn't require it. But she hasn't forgotten the paths: those are etched inside of her, imprinted on her consciousness.

They must be near to Cross Bones now, she thinks, where the surrounding ground is marsh, the pits older, the magic thicker. She doesn't know what Catherine wants to do down here—what she needs this place for—but whatever it is, she could probably do it at Cross Bones. She shudders. She hasn't been there in a long time. The place doesn't have the best associations for her.

She can feel the pulse she's following speed up, a jarring warning that grates against her nerves, and then Francis is pushing past her, aiming for the slippery ladder set in the wall, light glimmering down from the opening above.

"Are you insane?" she hisses, grabbing at the back of his trousers, his anger crackling in the back of her mind. "There are—" She listens, letting the sounds only she can hear echo. "Something's wrong."

Francis stares at her, unblinking eyes reflective in the gloom. "She's close," he says, and her eyebrows climb toward her hairline.

"Excuse me?"

Francis cuts her off with a gesture, looking up. "She's close, I can—I can tell, I don't—"

"If you can tell where your sister is," Jamie hisses at him under her breath, "I'm not sure *why you hired me*—"

"I didn't—I couldn't," he says, looking perturbed. "But it's like—I don't know, this kind of sixth sense, and she's so close—that I—I—"

"Fine," Jamie says, giving up as she watches him start to climb the ladder. She seriously debates just leaving him to it if he's so sure, but she can feel some kind of disruption fizzling in the air that isn't coming from him. Jamie has only been up all the way into the sanctuary beneath Cross Bones once, but it's a powerful spot: it's unconsecrated, which means nothing at all to Jamie, but meant to great deal to a multitude of the dead housed there. Jamie prefers other options, but she isn't so discerning that she won't go in.

She sighs and clambers up the ladder, but she doesn't get further than the third slippery rung before there's a crash, the sound of bodies hitting the ground, and a sudden sense of stillness from Francis before something changes. There's a subtle shift in her awareness that she can't put her finger on, and then a low, inhuman growl.

Jamie pushes herself faster, heaving herself into the small space with little dignity but speed enough to make up for it, only to have to dodge a fist immediately. She kicks blindly, connecting with a kneecap purely by chance. Her assailant falls over and hits his head on something, letting out a groan, and stops moving.

She rolls out of the way before he can get up again, trying to parse what she's seeing, figures illuminated hazily by the narrow window cut into the ceiling.

In the space of a few ragged breaths, Francis has gone, and in his place is something she doesn't recognize. Dripping lips draw back over huge white teeth, fur rippling into place where before there was only skin and wet fabric. He isn't a dog, or a wolf, or a big cat, but some unholy mixture of the three. An animal designed to commit violence.

A second man, closer to Francis, starts to laugh. He's got intimidatingly broad shoulders and a shock of black hair, and as Jamie watches something seems to move under his skin. "Fancy meeting you here," the man says. "You gonna fight me, Fran? You know, we should be on the same side here."

The thing that was Francis growls from where it's pressed against the ground, looking up at the man standing in front of him.

"You were never much of a brain though, were you?" The man's voice has started to get strange and Jamie realizes it's because his jaw is beginning to extend. She glances over at his unconscious companion, who still isn't moving, and tries to figure out which would be the least suicidal plan of action: stay or go.

Francis growls and the man laughs. "Besides, I don't think you're really in fighting form right now. Isn't that right?"

The rest of the change happens so fast Jamie almost misses it: fur rippling over his broad biceps, his forearms, his thick neck. And then there he is, heavier than Francis; bigger, bristling.

She starts to edge back toward the ladder—maybe she can pull up some kind of glamour to throw them off the scent, or maybe they'll decide she's not worth the time, and just go after Catherine instead—when the man next to her lets out another groan, rolls over, and grabs her leg. She tries to shake him off, looking over her shoulder when she hears a thud. The two beasts on the other side of the crypt are rolling across the wet ground, so quickly and so fluidly she can barely tell which is which. She tries to pull her leg away, kicking wildly, and feels something coil tightly around it. When she looks back, alarmed, she see what appears to be part of a modestly sized python sliding around her calf. The man looks up at her and grins, teeth bloody, eyes crossed. He's short one arm but otherwise appears to be in fighting form.

"Jesus fucking Christ," she chokes, and sticks her fingers in his eyes.

Across the crypt, the creature she thinks is Francis gets tossed against the wall. The other one lets out a growl—*Well, that's that*, Jamie thinks faintly as she keeps trying to push the man—well, sort of—off of her. *I'm going to get strangled by an arm-snake.*

But Francis pushes the other—thing—back, letting out a low roar, toppling him over, and in a movement that happens so fast Jamie almost misses it, sinks his teeth into the other creature's neck.

The blood spray is so bad some of it even reaches her, all the way across the chamber. Francis growls. "Oh, *shit*," the man currently squeezing the life out of her says, and she's suddenly released, flopping to the ground with a gasp, as he twists and shifts from—whatever hybrid thing he was—to another mammalian predator, but not in time. He isn't finished before Francis is done with him. When she turns to look at his body she wants to throw up. She has a pretty flexible attitude about what is and isn't natural, but that—that doesn't seem to qualify.

She watches, fascinated, as Francis shakes himself off and ripples again, heartbeat changing as he elongates. In the space of seconds he returns to a washed-out human form, clothing misshapen but somehow not gone, eyes fever-bright and reflective, panting heavily.

"Well," she says. "What the fuck was that?"

"Is she gone?" he asks, and she stares.

"I don't know," she says, staggering to her feet and spreading her arms expansively. "Do you think she could possibly have noticed that something was going on here?"

He looks around at room, which is full of pooling blood and distorted bodies, and then glances up at the sliver of light coming through the ceiling. "Well," he says. "How do we get out of here?"

As soon as Jamie drags them out of the tunnels, Francis staggers to the side, every breath dragging at his throat as though it's still not quite the right shape inside. His feet slip on the mud sloping up from the side of the river.

He doubles over, pain impossible to ignore, like jagged glass working its way out through healed-over skin, tearing at his insides, whatever space they might be occupying now, in whatever configuration. It's been weeks since he's had this kind of facility in his own body, not since he felt the space between him and Catherine first stretched out thin by distance, almost but not quite worn through. Been weeks since he's felt that natural. But now it's all gone again, and his body seems to be rapidly paying for it, shrinking in on itself as though it was never supposed to have done any of this, bones seizing up, muscles clenching, organs under siege.

The brief high of the change has vanished, replaced by the after-effects of what he had used it to do. His stomach roils again. He can still see them in front of him, their bodies on the ground. Worse, actually: he can taste them. His teeth are shaped differently now than they were twenty minutes ago but there's still blood sunk in the gaps between them. He turns and throws up.

Jamie doesn't look much better, dark skin gone ashen from dust mixing with sweat. She tactfully steps aside, moving up the riverbank, looking for a ladder. The tide is still low but rising. Its briny smell feels surprisingly clean compared to the rest of the city, which to him smells too strong and too unnatural, a glut of overlapping scents vying for prominence.

She comes back with a lit cigarette, composure seemingly regained, and the smoke alone is enough to set Francis' nerves jangling. He doubles over again, unsure if he's going to vomit on his shoes.

"The fuck is wrong with you?" Jamie asks, cigarette smoke streaming from her nose as she speaks.

"Put that thing out," Francis manages, voice coming thick.

Jamie shrugs and flicks it away into the mud, crouching down for a better look at him. "You all right?"

"Do I look all right?"

"You look like shit."

That in itself should be worrying, but Francis can hardly think through the haze.

He can't hear anything past the rush of blood in his ears, the thump of his own heartbeat deafening in the silence. He can't avoid thinking about it anymore: there's something wrong with him. There is. His physical body has always been the thing he's been able to count on, the vessel through which all else is channeled, the paradoxical shifting constant of his life. But this: this is wrong. This isn't just fatigue, or illness. This is something else. Something is wrong. *I don't think you're really in fighting form right now.* He shudders.

Jamie is still looking at him, eyes creased from exhaustion, skin gone a darker purple beneath them. There's still mud on her boots from the tunnels she'd dragged him into and then fought to drag him out of, her hair coming out of its twist to catch the orange glow of the streetlights.

She's waiting for him come to a decision. Part of him wants to punch her for dragging them underground in the first place. If she hadn't, then he wouldn't have—he would never have—he shakes his head to clear it. Maybe he would punch her, if he didn't think breaking the skin of his knuckles over her teeth would be the worst thing he could possibly do right now.

"We should keep going."

Jamie laughs, an oddly mournful sound for the expression on her face. "After that?" She sucks in a breath, hands resting on her thighs, head hanging down between her arms for a moment before she uncurls, sweat beading on her upper lip. "You fucking kidding me? Out with it."

"Out with what?"

"What the hell was that in there? Who were those guys? In case you didn't notice, one of them almost crushed me by turning into some kind of—snake tentacle, I don't fucking know. And they sure seemed to know you."

Francis lets out a heavy sigh. "They were—family members."

She looks at him expectantly. "And?"

"Cousins," he says tersely. "We grew up together."

Marcus and Otis and Silas and Cassius and Elias and Cyrus and Amos: The Cousins, as he and Catherine referred to them collectively. He and Catherine had spent their entire childhood bickering, sniping at each other, always at each other's throats, but they had always been a united front against The Cousins. The pair of them were the babies of the family.

The clan, their mother had often explained to them, had once been vast, sprawling. Now, things were different: the family was a compact unit, and there was no escaping the seven boys who had made their childhood a misery. For a long time Francis hadn't even been sure if they were brothers or cousins themselves: they were simply a single unit of controlled terror. Marcus used to bait him into fights and then laugh as he batted Francis down almost effortlessly, no matter how big or strong Francis got, until he was old enough to know better. And now he's dead.

"And you're all killing each other because…?" Jamie asks.

"I don't know," he says gruffly. "I'm not sure what's going on. They—they were trying to hurt her. I could tell."

"So you're a psychic now," Jamie says, unimpressed. She doesn't understand. There's a way that animals behave that goes beyond intellect and psychology. It's all in the body, sweat-smells, sounds: and Francis lives in the body. It's what he knows.

"No," he says. "I just knew."

"Well," she says, huffing out a breath. "I can tell you this. She knows you're going to find her. She—I think she kind of wants you to, actually."

He blinks, looking at her. "Catherine?"

"Yeah, who the hell else do you think I'm talking about? *Catherine*. I think she… I don't know. Baited you out here for some reason. Like she's waiting for you to track her down. If she really wanted to drop off the grid permanently I'm pretty sure she could have. There are better places to choose than *here*."

He isn't sure what to make of this. He can't imagine putting this much effort into getting away from somebody— from Catherine—all in the service of ultimately getting close to her again. But Catherine has always been smart in ways that he isn't. He can't expect to understand what she's planning until she explains it to him herself.

"So, I figure I'm about done with this," Jamie continues. "She's not trying that hard to hide, and if what I saw back there is any indication, I'd say you could just find her yourself. Aren't dogs meant to have good noses?" She pauses, pulling her lower lip between her teeth. "I'm not putting myself on the line like this again until you tell me what's in it for me. There are a few ways I wouldn't mind dying, and getting crushed by a giant snake is not on that list."

He takes a breath, closing his eyes. There's light coming in through the thin membranes of his eyelids, turning them a dark red; a pulse of exhaustion in his temples; and the filthy taste of blood and mud is mixed on his tongue. But beyond that, beneath it, is a flutter of unease, a creeping cold from the center of him that's slowly icing over everything else. "I can't—" He can't look at her yet, still turned inwards. "I don't know why, but when she left I—I started changing."

He opens his eyes, unsure of what he's going to see, which lens he'll be looking through, but he feels all too human and all too fragile to be anything else.

Jamie snorts, unimpressed. "Aren't you meant to do that? Seems to me there's been more smoke than fire there, for what it's worth."

Francis has never been useless in a fight before, has never had to fight with his body for anything more than greater height, greater speed, greater weight. Now, he can barely trust himself to bite without losing teeth, and the sudden jerk of Catherine's proximity only to lose her again has dragged at him, left him aching in a way he never has before. All of it together is a slap; a real, true metric of how little time he has to find her and ask her to tell him again while he has ears to listen.

"I think… the longer she's gone, the worse—I'm getting weaker." He grits his teeth, grinding enamel until his jaw creaks. "I can't explain what it's like, losing control like this. It's like I'm fading. It only—it only started when she left."

"I'm not going to keep helping you hunt someone down just so you can get your—I don't even know what to call it!" She jabs at him, pointed finger stabbing into his chest before he grabs her wrist, pushing her off. "I'm going to need more than that."

"What I'm paying you isn't enough?" Francis is raw, unbalanced; the world shifts abruptly, and he looks down at her with sharpened eyes, every pore and hair and bead of sweat standing out in high relief. His claws are begging to burst from his fingers, stymied only by pain and exhaustion. The accusation twists at his gut. He isn't just trying to find Catherine for his own benefit. Is he? "I hired you to do a job."

Jamie doesn't step back. Instead, she presses in closer, hitches herself higher, lips peeling back from her teeth.

"You hired me to look. You don't get to tell me I have to do anything more, and you don't get to tell me I can't leave you high and fucking dry, and you damn well don't get to tell me any amount of money is worth me keeping on after a woman being chased by someone who just wants her back because oh no, his little claws are gone!" She grabs him, dragging his face towards her. "You don't want to press me."

In the space between breaths, Francis feels hot, a prickle in his veins all the warning he has that he's stepping close to something dangerous, barely held in check.

Francis shoves her, managing to get her to arm's length before she starts coming at him again, a sick tug in the bottom of his stomach all the warning he gets before she's back in his face. "I'm—if I don't find her, we're both dead," he snarls. He steps further out of her reach, breathing hard, flushed with anger and admittance both. "I'm dead, all right?" As soon as he says it, he knows it's true. There's something sick lurching in his stomach, in his veins. Catherine knows something he doesn't, something about him, about what's happening, and the longer she stays away, the worse it gets. And besides, what other option does he have? Slinking back home to his mother?

"So she wants to be found," he admits. "Fine. She's doing a pretty good job staying hidden."

"Well that's your problem, isn't it?" Jamie says. "I feel bad for you, but I'm not about to die for this. I've got other things to worry about. For all I know she's leading you around on some sadistic wild goose chase on purpose, and I'm not getting involved in that." She sighs. "Look, I'll take you back to The Stag. Since Jack sent you to me I assume she's feeling generous toward both of us at the moment, although God knows why. Maybe she can help you out. She'll certainly be more useful than sitting around staring at the walls of that empty flat, I can tell you that much."

"Fine," he says, voice dull. It's not her business anyway, really. He probably shouldn't have brought her in at all. It's a family matter. If Marcus and Otis showing up here chasing down Catherine have proven anything, it's that. But he won't have a pleasant time figuring this out on his own, especially not when his entire body feels like it's on the verge of failing. "Let's go."

When they cross the neutral threshold of The Stag, Jamie audibly chokes on the air. Francis can see why: the entire room is a mess. He steps over a broken glass to avoid grinding shards into the rug, though he doubts it will make much of a difference in the long run. The place was filthy the first two times he was here, even to his dulled senses, but it had lacked the liberal application of splintered furniture exploding out from the center of the room and the splatter of blood coating the walls that now dominate the room. The air smells electric, the static hanging around still enough to bring his hackles up.

"What the hell happened here?" Jamie asks, skirting a splintered chair.

"How kind of you to stop by," says the dark-haired woman sitting behind the bar: Jack, Francis thinks. The huge blonde woman next to her is holding a rag to her eye, blood streaking her white hair red.

"I take it you came out on top," Jamie says looking around, and Jack smiles, all teeth.

"As it were."

"I've brought this one back," Jamie says, jerking a finger over her shoulder. "We seem to have hit a stumbling block. But it looks like you might have bigger problems on your hands."

"In fact," Jack says, "our problems happen to be the same problem."

Francis sucks in a breath as Jamie goes tense beside him. "I didn't bring whatever this is down on you," she says. "You're the one who sent him to me in the first place."

"And look at how much good that's done me," Jack retorts. Her black hair swings over her shoulder as she pinches the bridge of her nose. There's a spray of blood drying on the side of her neck, smeared where she must have wiped the rest from her face.

Francis shifts on his feet, trying not to betray how uncomfortable he feels. He hadn't known, when he'd come here, how much was going to happen as a result: he'd just been going to a bar someone told him to check out, in case somebody could help him. *It's the place everyone goes, when they need… you know. That sort of thing.* So he'd come, and the tall one, white-blonde and terrifying, had silently served him a drink when he sat down and started talking, lulled by the nominal safety of the place. *I'm looking for someone. I've never been here before. I don't have a lot of time.* She had disappeared, and the other woman had come back in her place. *I've got just the person for you*, she'd told him, with a smile that in retrospect he should have known meant trouble.

Jamie laughs, a strange, brittle sound, very different from the low chuckle he's heard from her before. "Since when do you send me business, Jack?"

Jack looks at her very coldly. "I wouldn't complain, *Jamie*. You know you stand on very thin ice here. You want to repay the debt? This is how you start."

Jamie shifts from foot to foot, hands going deeper into her cavernous pockets before she answers. "I'm—all right. Fine. *Thanks.* What do you want?"

Jack looks behind Jamie at Francis, gray eyes an uncomfortable weight. Francis can see why having this woman against you would be a mistake, and wonders what Jamie did to manage it. He is uncomfortably reminded of his mother. Or, more accurately, of being in the same room the few times

Catherine had stood up to her, instead of just witnessing the aftermath.

He swallows and looks away.

"This one's looking for his sister." Jack jerks her chin at him before looking back at Jamie. "He's not the only one, as I had the pleasure of discovering earlier today."

Jamie snorts. "Yeah, we know. It looks like you handled yourselves just fine."

Jack smirks. It's not a pleasant expression, but there's something compelling about it, a kind of seductive danger. Francis fights the urge to back up. "Well, not quite," she says. "One of them just *happened* to get away."

"Just happened, huh," Jamie says.

"I may have let him get away," Jack says mildly. "I don't take too kindly to people doing… this… to my pub."

"And?" Jamie asks expectantly, sounding amused. Francis, watching them, feels as though he's missed a step. They talk to each other like there's an entirely different conversation they're having below the surface, to which nobody is privy but themselves.

Jack gestures behind her, and the tall, blonde one hands her a glass, congealing blood settling in the bottom. Jack takes it, her short fingers leaving more streaks on the outside. "I thought you might… do us all a favor."

"Of course," Jamie says sourly. "Why wouldn't I?"

"I can't imagine," Jack says, tone suddenly icy. "Why wouldn't you, Jamie?"

Jamie doesn't say anything more, just takes the glass, tapping her fingers against the side. Jack has turned, swiveling on the bar until she's looking at Francis, pinning him from paces away. "You. Just be glad I don't like it when out-of-towners think they don't have to play by the rules. Despite how it may appear, we do our best to keep a low profile out here"—Jamie snorts—"and I'd appreciate it if you'd both *keep your heads down.*"

"Not much you can do when people are trying to kill you, is there," Jamie mutters, staring down into the glass of blood.

Francis doesn't respond at all, just stares straight ahead as though everything that's been said in the last twenty minutes has washed over him and left nothing behind. Jamie elbows him, bone catching bone as she hits him in the ribs. He startles, jerking back. "Don't do that."

"Haven't got anything to say about this?" Jack's eyebrows are raised. "I'd imagine you'd have some idea who's chasing you around London and nearly killing people in the process."

Francis gives himself a shake, smoothing a hand back through his overgrown hair as he takes a pained breath. "I don't know why they're—I don't know," he lies, and tries not to show it. Next to him, Jamie looks at him out of the corner of her eyes, and then back down into her glass.

"Really," Jack says, voice flat.

"Apparently so," Jamie says, almost cheerfully, and Francis can't help feeling relieved as she suddenly tips the glass back, blood pouring down her throat.

☞

Francis watches Jamie pick her way across London with a kind of fascinated horror. Over the past hour and a half, she's hopped turnstiles, yanked rusty gates aside and climbed barricaded fire escapes, finally ending up where they are now, crouched on a rooftop looking down at an unremarkable street.

She hasn't said much. He can hear her breathing next to him, a silent, bony presence. A part of him feels like he should apologize, though he's not sure what exactly for. Or thank her, maybe. He isn't sure why she's here leading him along—what it is about Jack asking that's so compelling—but it's a relief.

Where *here* is remains unclear, though. He looks around the grimy streets with a frown. They're in a part of town he doesn't recognize, although that doesn't mean much. "Are you sure this is—"

Jamie holds up a hand, eyes closed. Alfie had recoiled when Jamie had taken the blood in The Stag, wearing a slightly repulsed expression. Francis, who can still recall every unsettling detail of Jamie's face when she had taken his, hadn't been startled by the colorless wash of her eyes, although he hadn't entirely been expecting the shudder that had gone through her before she'd handed the glass back with no loss of composure, saying it was a nice change from his own on the way out. It hadn't been nearly as dramatic as her collapsing on the floor, unconscious.

He thinks about Catherine as they walk. She used to spend hours practicing shifting her face, perfectly mimicking Marcus or Cassius or Uncle Gordon, which always terrified everybody, including Uncle Gordon himself. She practiced using complete strangers, on the rare occasions that they encountered them: she could become anybody from a child they'd seen from a distance to a miniature facsimile of their mother, which was the only thing that could truly unsettle him. Francis, like most of the family, was a creature of fur and paws and claws: a creature of the earth. In some ways, he thinks now, Catherine never really belonged: she had all of their mother's viciousness but seemed somehow more human than the rest of them. She could not escape her body.

As a rule, Francis has very little interest in people, instead occupying himself with the shift of seasons, the drift of sand on the breeze, the structured turn of a wing. Now, though, he's been suddenly confronted with someone whose existence differs radically from his own, whose feet are only accustomed to concrete and river mud, and he finds himself wondering where she came from, whether she sprang fully formed from a doorway only few people ever see, or if she has a family somewhere who don't know what they've produced. These are the sorts of questions Catherine used to ask, not him. Catherine, he thinks, would have been fascinated by Jamie. His family always warned him about the world, but he wonders now whether he should have had that education.

"He's on the top floor, I think." She moves from a crouch to sit cross-legged on the flat roof, heedless of the accumulated grime of pollution on the cladding, glancing at him sidelong, evidently in no rush. "So, who are these cousins of yours? I'm not exactly in the market for secrets, but if I've got to do this, I may as well know what I'm getting myself into."

Francis shifts awkwardly, linking his arms around his knees. "My family wasn't... that big," he begins hesitantly. "Not compared to what it used to be like, anyway. And we all lived together. More or less. We have some land. Some territory. Have for a long time."

He takes a deep breath. "Catherine and I were—are—the youngest. The others—there were seven cousins, from—you know, an uncle and a cousin once removed, it didn't matter, we all grew up together. But they were all older than we were. So..." He trails off, trying to figure out how to phrase it.

"They made your lives hell," Jamie finishes for him.

"Yes," he says ruefully.

"I grew up being shunted around from home to home all over London," she says. "All kinds of aunts I'd never heard of, that sort of thing. There were lots of cousins. Kids are fucking awful."

"Well," he says, "Marcus was the oldest one. I guess it makes sense he'd come. And Otis was his brother. He was always… weird."

"Marcus the one you offed?" Jamie asks. "Well, I guess you offed both of them. But—"

"Yes," Francis interrupts. "We used to practice changing—compete—who could go faster, change into the most things in the shortest amount of time. Marcus and I were the best. And Otis did this thing where he… just made part of himself… something." His face twists. "I never really understood how."

"You couldn't do that?" Jamie asks, curious.

"I wouldn't want to," says Francis, honestly. The very idea makes his skin crawl. There had always been something slightly unsettling about Otis. A kind of glassy-eyed look. Once he had made all the fingers on his left hand into slugs. Catherine always thought he was funny. Francis decidedly did not.

"What about the rest of them?" she asks.

"There are seven. All boys. Men, I guess. I don't know how many of them came," Francis says. "I guess they—killed some of them. Marcus and Otis were brothers, and Silas and Cassius, and Elias and Cyrus and Amos."

"Well, that's a lot of variety," Jamie mutters.

"I don't know what they'd do without Marcus," Francis tells her honestly. The cousins had always been nightmarish to deal with but Marcus had been the worst, goading them on to catch up with his more sadistic tendencies. He was the biggest and the strongest, and cleverer than everybody except Amos, who was the youngest of the seven, and the most anxious. Being clever hadn't stopped him from falling into line as he was supposed to, of course. It had probably only made things worse for him, Francis thinks now. "What can you tell about—whoever's in there?"

"Not much," Jamie says. "He's nervous."

Well, Francis thinks, that doesn't say much. Anyone would be nervous.

He thinks about what he's done: thinks about all of those years growing up next to them, Marcus and Otis, no matter how much he hated them, and the fact that now he's the one who's killed them. The animal brain makes it easier, as simple as shaking the life out of a rabbit, but the feeling after, the creeping nausea and the lingering blood—that had been new; harsh and unwelcome. It's still lingering. He thinks it might linger for a long time.

"Why are they trying to kill you?" Jamie says. "Just so I have all my facts straight, before we go in here."

Francis thinks. In some ways, it seems like the logical conclusion of their lifelong relationship. They've always hated each other, and the rules of life where he comes from are more inclined to violence than they are here. But if he thinks—

"They must be trying to usurp clan leadership," he says wearily, and Jamie just looks at him as though he's speaking Greek. He sighs, and tries to think of a way to explain it without sounding ridiculous. It isn't ridiculous—it's more serious than she could possibly imagine. "Look—we have this territory, this land, and the family has lived there for—a long, long time. Clans fight over territory all the time, and you need to have enough strength to… push back threats. Other shifters." He tries not to shudder at the thought of what he's had to do in the service of the family: the many nights his mother had sent him out to the edges of the land, *To defend us.* Coming back with his mouth stained red. *It was necessary,* he tells himself. It was necessary.

"The more people in the clan, the more powerful it is," he continues. "The magic is more—dense, I guess. More connected. And the head of the clan is always a woman."

"Well, isn't that forward-thinking," Jamie says, and he huffs out what might, in other circumstances, be a laugh.

"When the clan is big, you have more people to draw from," he explains. "When it's small… you don't. So…"

"Catherine's it," she finishes. "And I assume that hasn't stopped your delightful cousins from wanting to bump her off?"

"Apparently not," he says sourly. "One of my uncles probably sent them." He thinks of Uncle Gordon, Marcus and Otis' father, who had once held him underwater until he grew gills—"For your education, boy!"—and his face twists. "I had one uncle who was—particularly unpleasant. If one of them had had a daughter, then maybe they would have just— fought over it, but—"

"God, this is a clusterfuck," Jamie says, tapping her fingers against the roof. "Can't you just go live in cabins in the woods or something? Seems like it's not hardly worth the trouble."

Francis blanches. "No," he says. "It's—having that territory—it's not just land where you live, it's—it *means* something. You can—feel it, somehow. It's not like just buying a house."

"Sure," she says, dubiously. "Well, I guess your sister got over that one."

He doesn't say anything: it appears to be true.

"Come on," Jamie says, standing up. "This has been great, but I think it's about time to go find this fucker."

"When you put it that way," Francis mutters, and Jamie grins at him sharply as he pushes himself up. He pauses a moment, taking a few breaths.

"You doing all right there?" she asks, and he waves her away. He'll be fine, he thinks. He managed it last time.

Jamie peers down over the roof. The sickly glow of neon signs from the street paints green highlights on the contours of her face, eyes shadows as she looks away. "Well, what's the plan?" he asks.

"Now is usually when I call my client and tell them where to find whoever they're looking for," she says, lips twisting wryly. "I can tell you this much—you're going in there first, because I'm not about to go in blind after the shit I saw earlier."

Francis is still exhausted—he wants to do nothing more than lie down on this very roof and sleep, but he can't exactly argue with her. "That seems fair," he says.

"All right, killer," Jamie mutters. The words are clearly intended as sarcasm, but they cut into him sharply anyway. After all, she's right.

"Hopefully not again," he mutters.

"Right. Well, after you," she says, gesturing, and he takes a shaky breath and lowers himself down onto the balcony, landing as soundlessly as he can, which unfortunately isn't very. He winces, crouching next to the door, as Jamie comes down behind him, much more softly despite her heavy boots.

There's no stir of reaction from inside the flat, so he slowly uncurls, trying the window sash. It's getting colder, autumn edging towards winter, but it isn't the kind of cold Francis is used to, not the kind of icy northern winter that freezes your teeth. Jamie, of course, seems immune to it, wrapped in all her layers.

The window is locked. Jamie rolls her eyes and fishes around in her cavernous pockets, finally emerging with a pocketknife, and leans around him to unceremoniously jam the blade between the sash panes, twisting her wrist until the lock pops.

She puts the knife away and lifts the window, gesturing for Francis to go first. He does his best, but the space is small, and he catches on the sill, body not as responsive as it was even yesterday, let along hours ago. Now that Catherine's gone again, the brief window of energy she opened up and then closed again seems to have made him feel even worse: more brittle, clumsier.

Jamie shoves Francis the rest of the way into what turns out to be a kitchen and follows more nimbly behind him. They both stand frozen for a moment, listening. Francis doesn't know who will be here, who survived. He closes his eyes for a moment and takes a deep breath, twisting the deep tunnels of his ears: he can hear the scritching of mice in the walls, bugs running under the floor, the low murmuring of a couple arguing on the floor above. And nervous breathing down the hall.

She follows a step behind as he walks toward it, clenching and unclenching his fingers as he goes. He's not sure he could manage a full shift again. He can't do what Otis could but he can always bring out his claws. Hopefully that will be enough.

He stops in front of a door, breathing louder than ever, and shakes his head to clear it of noise. It takes a long moment for his hearing to return to normal, far longer than it usually would, but if he let it stay that way he'd be distracted by the mice and the bugs and the people fighting and the cars honking outside. He can tell Jamie's getting impatient behind him, so he takes a deep breath and pushes the door open.

Amos is sitting huddled against the opposite wall, curled in on himself, looking as small as Francis has ever seen him. There's a dilapidated couch stretched out between them and a couple of chairs under the windows on the opposite side of the room, but Francis has a clear path to him if he needs one—or vice versa.

Nobody says anything at first. Amos doesn't even look up, eyes fixed firmly in front of him: his knees are pulled all the way up to his chin and his long fingers are trembling where they're knotted together. His overgrown hair could use a wash. He's only five years older than Francis and Catherine, and Francis understands now that Amos must have been everybody's punching bag until he and Catherine came along. Then suddenly Amos became one of the older tribe, but it hadn't quite stuck. He never seemed to really belong with them either. He was a kind of limp, anxious person, who had made Francis anxious as a child: he was difficult to like.

Finally, Jamie pokes Francis in the back, and he starts out of his reverie. "Amos?" he says, and Amos presses his hands against his face. "Amos," he says again, "what the hell is going on? What are you doing here?"

"Go away," Amos says.

For a moment, Francis feels stymied. What, after all, is he supposed to say? *I killed Marcus? And Otis?* He can tell himself that he didn't have a choice—he can still see Marcus advancing on him, the change ready to burst through his skin—but that doesn't seem to make it much better. *Go away* is not a response one expects to hear in this type of situation.

"Why did you all follow me?" he says instead of any of the other things he might say, because he figures he has to say something.

"Go *away*," Amos says again.

"*Amos*," Francis snarls, almost in spite of himself, and Amos twitches.

"We were supposed to find Catherine," Amos says dully. "Gordon said—we were supposed to find her."

"And do what?"

Amos looks up at him finally. "What do you think?"

"*Why?*" Francis asks, even though he knows. He still can't quite believe it: it seems somehow absurd, impossible, like something that should be happening to somebody else.

"Gordon said—" Amos starts, and frowns, looking down at the cuff on his sleeve as he picks at it compulsively. "He said she didn't really want it if she was leaving. So she would be—a liability—"

"Why not just leave her alone, then?" Francis asks.

"You know that's not how it works," Amos says, looking up at him. "You know it's not. People don't just *leave*." Francis can't exactly argue with him. He's right. People definitely do not just leave. Not until now. Not until Catherine.

"So, what, he sent all of you over here?" Francis says, and Amos shakes his head.

"Cassius is at home," he says. "Just in case. Marcus and Otis wouldn't stay."

"Well, I guess that was a good idea," Francis says, an uncharacteristic note of sarcasm creeping into his voice.

"Are they all dead?" Amos asks, still staring at the cuff of his sleeve.

"Were they all with you?" Francis asks. "When you were trying to follow me—"

"We weren't trying to follow *you*, we were trying to follow Catherine," Amos mutters. "We—"

"Well you didn't do a very good job," Francis says. His hands are clenched into fists. He can hear Jamie breathing behind him. "Except Marcus and Otis, I guess."

"So they're dead?"

"Yes," Francis says. "They're dead." Amos, if possible, shrinks into himself even further, and then looks up at Francis, eyes gleaming strangely.

"You don't know," he says. There's something strange in his eyes. "There's stuff you don't know."

"What?" Francis says, confused. There are all kinds of clan secrets that only his mother knows, that Catherine may already have inherited—but that doesn't mean Amos would—

"They're fucking with you," Amos says. He's shifting now, nervous, as though he might spring up at any moment. Francis takes a half-step backward just as he closes his eyes. "They're playing a game with you. All of them. Us too. But you—you—"

"What are you talking about?" Francis asks, heart beating fast. "What the hell do you—"

"They're bad people," Amos says, opening his eyes. "They're bad people and they did a bad thing."

"What—" Francis says, but at that very moment Amos says, "Sorry," and raises up his hand, bursting with claws, and draws the sharp blades across his own throat.

⚜

Jamie's seen her fair share of disturbing things, and it's not as though the sight of blood generally gets to her. But her heart is still pounding as they crawl down the fire escape and hurry through a winding series of alleys and back roads that she's choosing almost instinctually. Francis, walking next to her, is as white as a sheet, and hasn't said a thing since that man—Amos?—killed himself. Jamie officially has no idea what the hell is going on, and she doesn't like it: doesn't like the fact that she's been dragged in and doesn't like the fact that she doesn't seem able to extricate herself.

She could just cast Francis off, now, vanish down one of these streets and leave him be, but that would feel wrong somehow. Cruel, after what they've both just witnessed, but also unjust in some obscure way, for all that Jamie's rarely concerned with justice. She can't say she exactly likes Francis but she certainly feels bad for him, and there's some elusive quality about him she still can't quite work out, as though there's some missing piece she hasn't quite managed to put her finger on. If nothing else, Jamie likes puzzles. She thinks she'd like to solve this one.

Besides, if she ditched him, she has a funny feeling someone would come banging down her door inside a week ready to rip her throat out, for reasons unknown.

"Come on," she says, once they're finally back on a main road. The sun has long since set by this point, the streets murky and dark. "I have a place we can go."

Sarit seems unsurprised to see them, but that's probably just because Sarit's never really surprised by anything. Jamie smiles a little sheepishly at her as she walks in the door. "Sorry," she says. "We've had an… interesting day."

"You certainly look it," Sarit says, eyeing their muddy clothes. "And smell it."

Jamie, who's become so accustomed to the raw smell of river muck that she's stopped noticing it, winces.

"Well," Sarit says. "I guess I should feed you both."

Francis doesn't say anything the entire time that Sarit's cooking—"All I've got in the cupboard is pasta and a jar of sauce and if you think I'm going out to get anything else at this hour of the night you're going to have to seriously reevaluate your worldview"—or while they eat. Sarit keeps up a steady stream of chat about her day but Jamie can sense her watching him. She's too tired to say or do anything about it. Sarit would probably be able to get more out of Francis in an hour than she would in a day, anyway. Especially since she feels like she's about to pass out.

"Can I get you anything?" Sarit asks him when they've all finished eating, and he's visibly startled when he realizes she's speaking to him. "Tea, something stronger?"

He stares at her. "Oh, um, no, thank you," he says finally.

"Well, I'm going to make some tea," she says, and turns to Jamie. "You?" But Jamie just shakes her head.

They sit there in silence while the electric kettle boils, Jamie staring at the ceiling and thinking about everything that's happened in the day. It seems impossible that it's only been one day: it seems like a week, if not longer. She's seen more people die today than she'd ever care to. She wonders if there's something Francis isn't telling her: wonders if he was expecting this host to descend upon them, and whether he knows what exactly his cousin meant when he said, *They're bad people and they did a bad thing.*

There's stuff you don't know, he'd said. But how much? Everyone's a liar—Jamie knows that better than most. The question is how evenly you balance your lies with the truth.

Sarit comes back with her tea. "I can make up the couch for you, if you'd like," she tells Francis.

"Oh, you don't have to," he says. "I can go back to the place I'm staying—I don't want to—"

"You look like you're about to fall asleep sitting up," Sarit tells him frankly, a note of amusement in her voice. You might as well." Francis does, indeed, look like he would collapse if he tried to get home on his own now, and there's no way she's going to escort him.

"Stay the night," Sarit says kindly, "and then you can figure out whatever you need to do tomorrow morning."

Francis lets out what might even be a low, mordant laugh. "Right," he says. "Thanks."

Jamie looks at him for a long moment and then turns her gaze back to the ceiling. She has some thinking to do, too.

She shivers, skin feeling tight and over-stretched, as though everything beneath it, all her multitudes of flesh and bone, are all reordering, pushing against each other beneath the membranes that should keep them discrete.

She gasps, and the sensation is gone, leaving behind a tingling numbness, starting in her fingers, her toes, the base of her skull where spine becomes junction, the cervical vertebrae more foramen than bone mass, a fragile conduit for the thick cord tethering consciousness to action.

She rubs her hands along her arms. She has to keep moving—they'll come back soon enough, always coming back. She has to go back and find the right spot, the perfect spot to do it, and hope Francis is smart enough to follow. She has to go back under the ground, back into the darkness—she can feel it pulling, pulling, pulling—

Jamie jolts awake, painfully aware of her limbs, one arm dangling off her small, rickety bed down to the floor, hand open as though reaching out for a handhold in the dark.

The paralysis fades, but for a brief, suspended moment, she's immobile before crashing back into her own body.

She rolls onto her back and folds her hands over stomach as she gazes up at the dark ceiling. There's only one person who might be able to answer any of her questions, aside from Francis, who doesn't seem likely to start talking, and may not know anything useful, anyway. She still can't quite work out why Jack would just send a client her way, even one as weird as Francis, unless there was something bigger going on. So there *must* be something bigger going on, something she hasn't managed to work out yet. She rolls out of bed and reaches around for her boots.

It's never a long walk to The Stag if she's going the right way. Her nerves have always been singularly resistant to soothing habits, but nevertheless, she smokes as she walks, and when she arrives, she lights another cigarette, turns on her heel, and paces back across the alley, flicking the butt over the neutral ground boundary. There are plenty of places with established neutral grounds in London—government offices, hospitals, St Paul's—where magic can be performed but only in certain controlled ways, but Jamie doesn't tend to frequent them, and the neutral ground at The Stag is something a little more personal, a little more idiosyncratic. It's all Jack. The whole pub, in fact, is Jack: Jamie doesn't think she's ever seen her outside of it.

She paces back and forth across the cobblestones, eight steps in either direction, glaring at what still looks like nothing to her most of the time.

"Fuck this," she says to the air, baring her teeth.

The boundary line says nothing back, unsurprisingly, but the two laughing women who shoulder past her give her as wide a berth as possible, looking askance at her from beneath their fringes. She grins back at them, enjoying the way they scuttle off in response.

Jamie sighs, takes a deep breath, and steps over. Perhaps predictably, nothing much happens. The cobblestones never do feel any different on this side, but everything seems to come into subtly sharper focus, even the wetness from the morning's rain taking on an odd shine where it's settled. "All right," she says to herself, "let's get this over with."

The door sticks in exactly the spot it always does. Jamie kicks it the rest of the way open and steps in as quickly as she dares, hoping her eyes will have a chance to adjust before she gets punched in the face.

"You've some nerve."

Alfie's black eye is gone, faded out overnight, and The Stag is back to its usual state, empty now that the last two patrons have left. If she hadn't been here not long ago, she'd never have known something had happened, but there's a lingering tang of electricity in air, just enough to tell her the cleanup crew's been busy. She'd have been on it once, Jack watching from the corner and never saying a word about free drinks. Jamie doesn't exactly know how many mundane authorities have tried to shut the place down over the years, but frankly anyone would have been doomed to fail if Jack was determined to keep it open.

Jamie rallies herself and smiles at Alfie, hoping it comes off as threatening. She's twice Jamie's size, so probably not. "Put in a good word for me, did you?"

Alfie snorts, putting her hands on her hips. "What do you think?"

"I think you'll die if you speak in full sentences." Jamie looks around. "I want a word with her."

"Want is such a strong word," Jack says, from her usual corner.

Jamie wishes she had her talent for hiding: she could have used it lately. She doesn't have Jack's gift for business, either, her endless mental tally of what's been bought and earned, of who deserved what information and who owes her what. She didn't realize, back when she and Jack were on good terms—better than good terms—how dangerous it was to be involved with somebody who never forgot a single favor she did for you, or anything you promised in return.

Jamie fights a grimace as Jack steps out from behind the bar, sliding into view. "Got a minute?" she ventures instead, aiming for charming. The simple fact of the matter is that she has no leverage—not a position she particularly enjoys. "My account's still open."

"I'd say it's gaining interest," Jack says. "What exactly brings you here at this hour of the morning?"

Jamie shifts uncomfortably. For all her determination, there's something about being in

Jack's presence that never fails to throw her off. This near, Jamie can't disguise the reaction she's always had to her, the natural attraction that she's half-sure is the effect of a glamour but probably has more to do with the way she responds to dangerous people who were, at one point, willing to fuck her. Jamie's never been picky and Jack's never been anything but what Jack wanted to be on a given day. Jamie wasn't even pretending she was in it for love: physical attraction was just a bonus to other things—other skills she realized she needed to learn too late to get them anywhere else.

"I need some answers," she finally says, a little more gruffly than she necessarily intends to, and bristles when Jack has the gall to look amused.

"I'm not sure you're entitled to answers," Jack replies.

"I need to know why you set me up," Jamie says baldly. "Why you sent him to me. You've been nothing but hostile to me for the past *year*—"

"I've barely *seen* you for the past year—"

"And now you send me a job," Jamie finishes, "that turns into the biggest clusterfuck I've ever worked on, which is saying something. That's not just chance. And don't tell me this was just charity, because I know you don't do charity, and I doubt you've suddenly started now."

"You'd never take it if it was," Jack says mildly, although her eyes are steely. She comes around to stand in front of her, blocking the door. She's five-foot nothing in bare feet, only slightly taller in shoes. Jamie's never been under the impression that her height would stop her doing anything unimaginably hideous to her if she wanted to. Jamie knows better, has seen what Jack has done to people who disrupt the oasis she's carefully carved out of London's chaotic maelstrom. "What happened?"

"We tracked down the last one," Jamie says. "The one you let go. It looked like he was alone. Some dirty little flat up north. He said something about some family infighting and then killed himself. It was fairly gruesome."

Jack smirks at her. "Nothing you're not used to, is it?"

Jamie chokes out an incredulous breath. "I didn't go around *murdering* people, Jack! I wouldn't—"

"Of course," Jack says, still smirking. "Besides, you're keeping yourself occupied with your little tricks now, aren't you? Nothing too fancy."

Jamie stares at her, incredulous. There are things she no longer does precisely because Jack made it very clear to her that continuing to do them would be a very bad idea, and Jamie, for all that she's always hated being told what to do, had known that she was right. There's a high every time she does her work, and consuming blood—the taste of it on her tongue, the thick slide down her throat—is an especially delicious thrill. But there are other ways and means of working with blood and all of them are a shock to the system. The rush of magic does something to her that nothing else has ever been able to—not drugs, not sex, not alcohol. Gives her a crackle under her skin. Makes her feel like some kind of god.

Jack was the first one who told her who she was: she still remembers it vividly, every word and gesture sharp in her mind. In bed, running one hand through Jack's smooth hair, other placed against her thigh, just above the blood pulsing through the artery beneath. Saying how well she could hear it, after having been inside Jack's body in a different way. Saying it with a smile, sure despite all the knowledge of what kind of fire she was burning herself with that it would be safe to lay a secret there.

She remembers Jack's nearly imperceptible stiffening, her careful release of each muscle until she could smile without looking strained, gently disentangling herself from Jamie's fingers. *So that's what you are*, she'd said, as though finally scratching an itch, unkinking a knot in her spine. *I was wondering.* And then everything in Jamie's life had changed. She doesn't regret it, of course. How could she? But she also can't exactly say she's better off now than she was before.

She is good at what she does: she's powerful. Jack had given her a place to sleep, taught her how to use what was already innately inside of her—and used her. Some part of Jamie had always known that she was being used, that their arrangement was unorthodox in a way that didn't necessarily benefit her. Jack brought her jobs and she did them and took whatever money she was given afterward happily. She'd had so little money before, from doing anything. It had seemed like an impossible gift. But Jack, as she would come to learn, was not someone who cared much, in the end, for anybody's interests but her own. Jamie supposes they're not much different in that way.

She'd done everything. She'd found people, bewitched them, misdirected them, consecrated ground, even once breathed life back into a baby that had died: that had been at the very end. She remembers that day all too well. Some kind of sudden death had taken it; it didn't much matter, for her purposes. Its mother had brought it to her, looking possessed. You couldn't bring somebody back without killing someone else. There were other spells people needed to die for but she'd never performed one, but this was a matter of simple equivalence: nothing else could give life. Jamie had explained to her and she'd claimed to understand. There were very careful instructions for how to get the baby back to her husband. They spent more than an hour arguing, but eventually Jamie had done it. It wasn't, she'd always argued to herself, murder. But she wasn't exactly sure what else she should call it.

She'd done it down in Cross Bones, in the dark. To do magic like that, you needed a worker like her and some other energy, some other kind of power. Part of her—the worst part, the part she usually tries not to think about—had been eager to see if she could surmount the challenge. She had. The baby had come back. Then, of course, she'd had to get rid of the body, and take the little girl back to her father. She's no good at glamours but she managed one that night, flush with the excess blood.

Sarit has told her time and again that Jack should have taught her better, should have explained to her the dangers of what she was doing and how she could control herself. But it wasn't in Jack's interest to do that, of course: the more Jamie did, the more Jack benefited. Jamie's never been as quick to blame her, though, at least not for that. The fact that Jack was the first person whose blood Jamie ever tasted, too young to know that she was being gauged and tested instead of properly taught and trained, makes her at least partially culpable. But Jamie was the one who let herself spin wildly out of control: Jamie was the one who let herself chase high after high, until she couldn't entirely parse the fabric of reality, until her very presence in The Stag was starting to shoot Jack's carefully established neutral ground to hell, until finally whatever power she had pent up inside of her exploded and created a scene not unlike the one here yesterday: furniture smashed, bodies unconscious on the floor, blood smearing the walls. At least nobody had died.

She would have sent herself away, too, after that. She effectively had. And she'd stopped doing almost everything but finding people. Finding people, she figures, is relatively harmless, even if some of them don't want to be found.

It isn't too hard to tell when people are looking for the wrong reasons. Mostly she just looks for cheating spouses. It's mundane work but that, she figures, is the idea.

Now, for Jack to be deriding her—she wants to shout, to scream, to list off every way in which she's wronged her. "I can't believe this," she says. "Are you kidding me? *You*'re the one who *banned* me—"

"I hardly expected you to pretend you're incapable of anything but tracking spells," Jack says, raising her eyebrows. Alfie, Jamie notices, is leaving out of one of the doors leading back to the kitchen. "I imagined that, at some point, you'd learn control, and then come to your senses. You owe me some work, in case you've forgotten."

"Maybe you could have helped with all that when you were making money off of me," Jamie snaps. "Maybe that would have been a little more efficient for both of us."

Jack just looks at her, long and impenetrable. It wasn't really all that long ago that even being this close to Jack would have been enough to turn Jamie's brain off, let herself be coaxed upstairs for a conversation and a drink and the heady slide of skin on skin, sweat and teeth and the thin edge of danger mixing into one maelstrom of desire Jamie has never been able to shake. But there was always, beneath it all, an ulterior motive: blood. Jack, Jamie thinks, sees people first and foremost as tools. And Jamie was a rare tool indeed.

"You told me," Jamie says, as calmly as she can, "that I—"

"Wasn't welcome on neutral ground when you disrupt it." Jack isn't shouting. She never shouts. She looks pointed. Jamie's always longed to pull something out of her that was more than torturously measured, even despite knowing from firsthand witnesses how bad it would have been if Jack had ever lost her maddening cool directly. "I stand by it. You know what your magic does here, and it upsets the balance. But that doesn't mean you couldn't learn to control it."

"I've been working on it," Jamie says, fingers clenching.

"I can see that." Jack looks at her appraisingly. "Have you got anywhere else to go?"

Jamie doesn't waste energy bristling. She has her little bed in the glorified closet that barely counts as Sarit's spare room, and Francis is unconscious on Sarit's lumpy couch. They're the only people who would wonder where she'd gone if she vanished, she thinks, and one of them would only care because she's got his blood running through her veins. The prospect is dispiriting.

"That's not why I'm here," Jamie says, and then can't help adding, "You're past caring, I thought." She may have learned not to raise her voice, but that doesn't mean she can't aim to cut.

Jack doesn't rise. Instead, the smile falls off of her strong-boned face, lines smoothing out until she's as ageless as she's always been, reptilian stillness evident for a fraction of a second before it's gone. "You know I don't like for The Stag to be disrupted, yeah?"

"Doesn't seem to put you above making a scene."

Jack smirks; fleeting, but there. "Everybody's got to have fun." She sobers, leveling a stare at her. "You've kicked up some dust with this one."

"I don't think it's exactly *me* who's kicked up dust," Jamie points out, but she's too tired to argue anymore. "Are you going to tell me why I'm back here, or should I just go?"

Jack hums a little behind her breath, walking around to the back of the bar and picking up a cloth. "You ever think he might have been running as well as chasing?" she asks as she starts to clean one of the glasses Alfie's left dripping.

Jamie stares. "No," she says, pushing a stool out of the way and leaning forward. Across town, Francis jolts awake, timing abrupt as her attention turns to his confusion, his immediate panic. "What do you mean?"

"Oh, nothing," Jack says, in a tone of voice that strongly suggests otherwise. "His family used to be bigger. They used to… travel more. You might say."

Jamie stares at her, skin practically vibrating. "What do you mean? Did you know them?" Jack doesn't look much older than forty but it would be impossible to pinpoint her exact age: Jamie's tried. She's tasted her blood and knows she's not quite human, knows she's old, inhumanly old—possibly even incomprehensibly old, but she doesn't know what exactly that means, in real terms. Anything past a few hundred years is history; anything past that is ancient, and beyond the scope of a practical imagination.

"This place has been around for some time," Jack says, which of course Jamie knows. That's an understatement. It's been around, effectively, forever. "I've seen a lot of people come through. And I don't forget faces. Their father was from around here," she adds. "Their mother met him here and carried him off, if you will."

"What was she doing here?" Jamie asks, and Jack shrugs.

"Maybe she wanted some new blood," she replies. "He was from an old family, though they've mostly died out now. Not enough land left." She pauses. "You know how those clans work, don't you? How the family hierarchy works?"

"I have some idea."

"Well," Jack says calmly, setting one glass aside and picking up a new one. "Their mother—your new friend and his sister's—had an older sister, from what I understand. Who would have been the leader of their clan."

Jamie waits, but Jack doesn't say anything more, just keeps drying the glass. A chill runs down her spine. "And…?" she prompts.

"Well," Jack says. "She killed her, obviously. I just thought you ought to know," she adds, with almost no feeling at all, "what you're dealing with."

"Great," Jamie snaps. "Thanks. Thanks for sending me this excellent job, I'm really grateful. If it kills me I hope you feel really satisfied at what you've accomplished. But you still haven't explained *why*."

Jack looks up at her and Jamie almost takes a step back. There's a cold look in her eyes that she doesn't like. "Do you really want to know? There are a lot of things I could tell you."

"Yes," Jamie practically shouts. "That's what I've been trying to—"

"You disappointed me," Jack says icily, and Jamie's jaw clicks shut. "You became boring. You cut yourself off from everything you're capable of doing."

"I didn't want to kill myself or anybody else," Jamie retorts, but Jack isn't listening to her.

"So I sent you something interesting," she continues, and Jamie goes still.

"How did you know that?" she says. Jack carefully puts the last glass to the side.

"This woman came in last month," she says mildly. "She was very... compelling. She told me her brother was going to come by looking for her. She figured he'd be through here, if he needed a little extra help." She smiles without warmth. "There aren't many places that offer what we offer, are there?"

"What—" Jamie starts.

"So," Jack says, "I told her I knew someone, but that it would cost her. She agreed to the terms."

"You *set this up*?" Jamie says. "You—"

"Well," Jack says, "she did."

Jamie's head is reeling; she can't decide whether to scream or sit down on the floor where she stands. Catherine has been lurking at the back of her mind for all these long woozy hours and she's felt her purpose, her attention to Francis, but—but—

"How did she pay you?" she asks, and Jack smiles.

"How do you think?" she asks. "Blood."

Jamie takes a long, shuddering breath. "It's valuable, coming from them, but I don't have to tell you that. I know you've already had some of her brother's," Jack says. "Which seems to have done the job. But you're welcome to have some more, if you like." She pauses. "Might get you back into the swing of things. I would have offered it up to begin with but I didn't think you'd have trusted it." She smiles, lips pressed together. "But you do seem to have lost your edge."

Jamie's fist curls. She probably shouldn't. She should just walk away, from Jack and from these people and their fucked up family and all of this blood. But Francis is in Sarit's flat and she can feel both him and his sister in her mind and under her skin, uncharacteristically persistent, and she's itching for it: for the kick. To know. *Where are you. What are you.* "All right. You win. I need it."

Jack stills, satisfied. She puts down the damp cloth and vanishes for a moment. Jamie leans against the bar, trying not to shake. She shouldn't be so bothered: in some ways, she guesses she knew already, but suddenly she feels like a rat in a maze, out of her league, worryingly outmatched. She's always been able to defend herself but she doesn't know the rules of this world. She doesn't know these people, or what she's embroiled in, and any additional bite will help, no matter where it comes from.

She stands back upright when Jack comes out carrying a stoppered bottle, straightening her shoulders. She watches as she turns over one of the glasses she's just dried, uncorks the bottle, and pours a finger of blood in, which slides slickly down the side. When she's finished, she sticks the cork back in the bottle, and pushes the glass across the bar.

Jamie reaches out, taking it and turning it between her fingers for a long moment before sighing. "What the hell," she says, and tips it back.

Her mind is a series of rapid-fire connections, an endless series of ricocheting particles of energy: she doesn't even need to ask *where are you*. Synapses are firing alongside her own; heartbeats aligning with hers. She is no longer a body but a sense. Catherine is sitting by the river, eyeing the drop. *Not the knees again.*

Her knuckles are bruised. She's impatient. There's only so much time. She needs to find the right one. The one with the right bones. She could call Francis again—she needs to convince Francis—but—Francis is sitting on Sarit's couch with a cup of tea. It's warm in his hands. Sarit's saying, *I've never been anywhere.* He's wondering if he should call Catherine again. He hasn't tried since she called him last. Maybe she's turned on her phone. *Jamie said she wanted me to find—*

Jamie gasps in a shuddering breath. Jack is watching her closely. "It's the same," she chokes out, before she can think better of it. "It's the same blood."

Jack blinks. "What?" she says.

"You just gave me the same blood," Jamie says, and Jack looks at her strangely. "I don't—I don't—"

Jack leans forward, light of avarice in her eyes, the promise of new information drawing her out, making her, briefly, seem warm. Safe. "Oh?" she says, voice low and sweet.

"I need to go," Jamie says, and slams out of the bar without even noticing the neutral threshold wobble as she crashes over it.

When Francis wakes up, he doesn't know where he is. He goes tense, heart pounding, squinting into the dark, until he remembers: Jamie's friend's apartment. He lies still for a moment and then pushes himself up, wincing. His body feels like it's aged a decade in the past two weeks, if not more. He peers around the room, trying to remember which door leads to the bathroom, when the woman—Sarit, he remembers—appears.

"Sorry," he mutters, guilty, "I didn't mean to wake you up—"

"I get up early," she tells him, waving a hand. "It's there. The toilet."

"Thanks," he says, removing himself.

When he comes back out she's got the light on in the tiny kitchen and is making more tea. "Don't suppose I can tempt you this time?" she asks, tone light.

"Sure," he says, and she gets out two mugs.

She hands his over and yawns as she walks back over to the squashed armchair next to the couch, settling in with a long exhaled breath. He follows, sitting down more gingerly next to her.

"Am I right in remembering that you were looking for your sister?" she asks, far too politely for this hour of the morning, as she sips her tea.

"Yes," Francis says.

"No luck?"

"Not exactly."

She lets out a little sigh and settles back into her chair. Her bleached hair glows luminously in the dim morning light. "Ever been to London before?"

He blinks. "No," he says.

"I've never been to America," she says. "I went to France once. Took a boat."

"I've never been anywhere," he says after a while, because he feels like he should say *something*. Besides, it's true.

She smiles a little. "I knew a shifter once," she says. "She'd sort of—left the tribe. You might say."

"Oh," he says, thrown off. "I—I don't know any shifters here."

"She—well, I suppose you could say she broke up with her family," Sarit continues. "Maybe divorced them. It was all rather unpleasant."

Francis swallows. "It sounds like it."

"I do family counseling," she explains. "In a sense. That's not how I knew her. But I've seen my fair share of family break-ups. It's not always a bad thing." She freezes, grimacing, but all her teeth are blunt, unthreatening. "I don't mean to suggest anything about your sister, of course."

"Right," Francis says, thrown.

"What is she like?" Sarit asks.

"Catherine?" He realizes that he's never really had to describe her to anyone. Everybody he's really known has already known her, before this week. "Smart. Argumentative." He pauses, trying to think of a diplomatic way to phrase *not always very nice*. "Opinionated."

Sarit smiles a little. "I know a few people like that," she says. "You'll find her. Jamie's good."

"We'll see." And then, a moment later: "What happened to your friend?" When she looks at him blankly, he adds, "The shifter. What's she doing now?"

"Oh," Sarit gestures with her mug, a few drops of tea sloshing over the side before she rights it with a twitch. "I don't know. I lost track of her. She was always very private, I suppose."

"Do you think she's happy?" he asks, hoping his voice doesn't betray the unease in his chest, tight and hard beneath the ribs.

"I don't know that anybody is *happy*," Sarit says. "I do think she made the right decision. Which is sometimes the closest thing. I think she's probably happier wherever she is than where she was."

He wants to ask: *What if you only know one place?* But he guesses this woman probably did, too, once, and still left. Like Catherine did. Like he did, too, though for a different reason. The tea is sitting on the crooked coffee table, giving off a scent he suddenly finds unpleasant; too rich, too warm to touch.

"I should go," he says, lurching up off the couch, joints protesting the movement, something heavy and cold seeming to settle in his bones. "I—thank you."

Sarit looks up at him, large eyes calm and considering. "Be careful," she offers. "Safe travels."

It feels, somehow, very final.

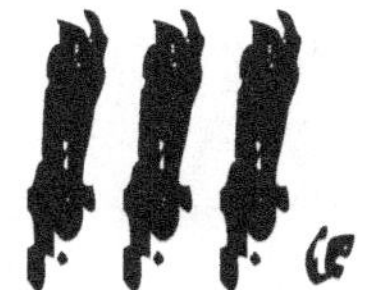

The city is waking up and he's nearly back to the building where he's been staying when his phone buzzes in his pocket. He fumbles for it frantically, heart pounding: he can't remember ever being this terrified of a phone call. When they were kids, the wall telephone in the hallway was off-limits, for emergencies only, and by the time they hit adolescence, Catherine had wanted one, a way to reach the outside world. She'd raged until she'd gotten her way, but Francis had never seen the point. She didn't wind up ever using it much. Who, after all, did she have to talk to?

He holds it to his ear without looking at the display, expecting to hear Catherine's voice, a dozen questions ready on his tongue. *What are you doing? What do you want from me? Why are you still running away?* But it's not Catherine who speaks.

"You've been busy, Francis," his mother says.

His breath catches in his throat, heart pounding so quickly he thinks she must surely be able to hear it down the line. He stops in the middle of an empty crossing, staring at the buildings across the way. "Mother."

"Is that any way to say hello? You've been gone a long time." Her voice is distorted: the phone's small speaker is probably beginning to corrode from all the rain and river water he's been trudging through over the last few days. It doesn't matter; he still has to listen.

"I'd hardly call this a long time." Francis' heart jumps in his chest, pulsing unpleasantly through his neck as he forgets to breathe. He swallows, tongue dry.

"Still. Imagine my surprise when I suddenly couldn't get through to you. It's not like you to be rude." No, it isn't. Of course it isn't. He's never done anything as bold as ignoring her, not even when he thought he was sick for the first time in his life, and asked her if she knew why.

Probably because your sister was selfish enough to leave.

He forces himself to at least walk to the sidewalk, muscles in his thighs bunching from tension. "I'm only doing what you asked me to."

"Are you?"

Francis doesn't answer. She let him go thinking that his task was going to be simple. Now he's here, and he feels ill, his body sluggish and failing, worse than his sudden paralysis after Catherine left. The cousins are nothing but dead bodies, now, and if Amos is to be believed, there's something about him that he doesn't know about or understand. He knows what his mother told him to do, but he no longer knows *why*, and for the first time, the why is important, a thread he has to follow.

He swallows. "Why did Marcus and Amos and all of them come over here?"

She doesn't say anything for a long moment. "Your uncle is a very foolish man, Francis," she answers, voice calm. "Unfortunately, it seems your cousins are as well."

"Were," he says. "They were. They're dead." A woman jogging with a dog passes by in front of him, close enough that he almost falls over, and he stumbles back to lean against the building behind him, one hand pressed against the brick.

"I see," his mother says after a moment's silence, and then hums, a sound Francis has only ever associated with displeasure. "You're going to have to take care of this girl you've been running around with, as well."

He goes still for a moment: he can see Jamie on the roof in startling detail, hair frizzed from the light rain earlier in the day, fingers twisted together as she watched him ruminatively, not saying much, just listening. He has no reason to trust her, no reason to defend her, but even so, something is in the way.

"I'll get it done," he lies, the bottom dropping out of his stomach.

"That's good, Francis," his mother says, in her soothing tone of voice that isn't soothing at all, but instead just makes his skin crawl. "Don't disappoint me."

"I won't," he mutters, and hangs up. He feels dizzy, world tilting sideways for a moment before it rights itself, and slowly pushes himself home.

He's barely been back five minutes when somebody starts hammering on the door. He stares, brows coming down. There's only one person it can be, he figures, unless his week is about to get much worse than it's been—which would really be saying something.

Jamie bursts through the door the second that he opens it, looking slightly manic. Francis can smell the magic on her—or he thinks he can almost smell it, acrid and coppery. Her chest is heaving and she's flushed as though she's just run from somewhere, which seems distinctly possible.

"Jamie," he manages, leaning back. "What's going on—"

She draws in a sharp breath and turns to stare directly at Francis. "You," she says. "Something's going on with *you*."

He stares, nonplussed. He feels like telling her that this isn't exactly news, but the weird energy vibrating around her is off-putting, so he just backs into the kitchen, letting her follow. "Has something… happened?" he asks, he asks, and she laughs a little, unpleasantly, eyes wide and unblinking, pupils blown all the way out.

"I had some of your sister's blood," she says, lurching into the room. "It's the same as your blood, did you know? Exactly the same."

"You saw Catherine? What—"

But she's shaking her head. "Jack had it. Apparently. She gave it to her in exchange for—services."

"What?" Francis asks, uncomprehending.

"That's right," Jamie says. "We seem to be knotted up in some *conspiracy*." She spits the word out like it's dirty. "I'm tired of it, aren't you? So let's go."

"Go where?" Francis skirts around her, unwilling to allow her any closer to him while he's still trying to process what she's saying.

"Go to your *sister*," she says. "I know exactly where she is. I know exactly where both—of—you—are." She steps forward, faster than he can dodge, and raps on his chest. "She's been waiting for you to come find her for days anyway. Evidently we just weren't clever enough. Or didn't do a good enough job getting past your murderous relations."

"Are you sure you're... all right?" She looks mad, the white of her eyes visible all the way around, even if they still have color to them, her stare fixed and rigid.

"I'm wonderful," she says, grinning with all her teeth. "Shall we?"

Francis wants to say no, but she turns on her heel as quickly as she lurched in, stepping off without stopping to see if he's following. He has to. It's his sister, his search, his blood.

❦

Francis follows her for what feels like hours, but blessedly, they're above ground, clambering out of a low wooden door set behind the watchman's house in a bucolic park, a setting so at odds with his mood that he blinks, surprised.

"Where are we going?" He wants badly to get a straight answer out of her, but knows better than to hope.

Instead, Jamie looks over her shoulder, frowning. "The throat," she says, which isn't an answer at all.

Francis, too tired to protest, just follows. One way or another, all this will be over soon. Jamie, ahead of him, skips over a knee-high fence and onto manicured grass, heading straight for a copse of trees, taller than any in the area, and a coiled part of Francis, at last, relaxes. The air may not be right, but the facsimile of nature is enough to give him a moment of calm before Jamie hauls the top off a little stone monument and stands on the rim, dark pit yawning beneath her feet. "It's a bit of a drop," she explains, and then she's gone, entering the belly of the earth as though it's nothing to her.

Francis has to fight to follow, but he forces himself to do it, feeling the channel brush the breadth of his shoulders before he's through and falling, only catching himself on his knees by pure chance. Of course, it would be too much to hope that they won't have to stay underground for long. Instead, Jamie sets off down another sloping path, shoulders rigid and stride mechanical, still drawn forward and down by something Francis can't see.

She isn't looking at him, so it's easier to think. He's never met anyone quite like her, in the sense that all the magic he's been exposed to has been carefully controlled, designed to maintain the balance without attracting too much attention. Jamie seems wilder somehow, despite being a creature of the city, mired in blood and centuries of displaced dirt. When she finally looks back over her shoulder, she catches him staring, her dark irises black in bright sclera, startling against the gloom.

He probably imagines the shiver that goes down his spine as Jamie looks at him, but then, his body isn't as trustworthy as it used to be. There's an itch on the back of his neck, a prickle deep in his jaw that might be new teeth erupting, eyes flicking through spectra before he takes a deep breath and fights the changes down.

Jamie jerks and stands still, pupils bleeding wide in the gloom.

Fittingly, Francis' blood—the thing that links him so strongly to a person whose presence has always set him on edge—runs cold.

There's a deep crevice in the wall, only visible from a certain angle, as though it has been hastily concealed, dirt and old stones obscuring its dimensions but not their passage. Jamie slides sideways and disappears, the murky color of her coat fading into the deeper gloom.

Francis follows by feel more than sight, skin crawling. They were never meant to be below the earth like this, he thinks, while still among the living.

Whatever he expects to find on the other side, it isn't Jamie standing stock still in a vast cavern, eyes shut, a nearly blissful expression on her face.

He swallows, fixated on her as the only familiar warmth down here, but unwilling to disturb her, not while she still wears this expression of almost possessed focus. Still, he has to know. "Is she here?"

Jamie opens her eyes. "This way," she mutters, heading into the darkness, path sloping ever so slightly down. Francis, in what's becoming a constant feeling, loses track of the turns, finding himself utterly dependent on Jamie if he ever wants to see daylight again.

Jamie takes a deep breath when they come to a bulge in the tunnel, not exactly the same as the previous two but a perceptible widening, nothing tangible marking the spot where he can already tell they're going to stop. He's flagging, but if he can't keep up, his odds will be even worse than if he just waits and lets her work. He takes a deep breath and leans against the wall, fingers shaking.

The last twenty-four hours have been something of a blur. Ever since he killed his cousins in the crypt, Francis has been drawn tight like a bowstring, and even if Jamie couldn't feel it, she'd be able to see it in the new lines on his face, in the way he walks as though he's not entirely sure he can trust his legs. Against her best judgment, Jamie is worried.

There's no point getting attached. She knows there isn't, but there's something inevitable about it, in its way. She's always managed to disentangle herself from blood before this, but her connection to him and Catherine and their uncomfortable overlap feels strangely intimate: they're both vibrating inside her in a way she doesn't recognize, and she has a drive to see this to completion that is utterly alien to her. Some of Francis' urgency is bleeding over, the most transference she's ever had from anyone. Her teeth are practically jittering from it.

"What are they?" Francis asks when they stop and he slowly lowers himself to the ground. "All this," he clarifies, when she looks down at him, uncomprehending.

Jamie blinks at him, amazed that after all this tramping around beneath the city he doesn't know. "They're plague pits, Francis." He stares past her, eyes glazed and distant. It takes a hung moment, a space between breaths, for her to realize he's not going to answer unless she prompts him. "I just don't know why would she need—" Jamie starts, but Francis interrupts.

"Our father was from London," Francis says, still staring into the distance. "I think. That was the story anyway. I never cared much."

Jamie crouches down to look at him, taking in the tightness around his eyes, the papery texture of the skin beneath them. That tallies with what Jack had said, which is confirmation, if not a comfort of any kind. Something begins to fall into place, in her mind. "Seems like an odd thing not to care about."

"We didn't know him." Francis doesn't seem keen to elaborate, but she waits anyway, to see if he'll keep going unprompted.

Jamie shrugs as best she can with her arms wrapped around her knees. "I didn't know my parents." There were only the myriad uncles and aunts, blood relatives and otherwise, who had taken her in from time to time, keeping her as long as they could afford, or as long as they could stand to endure her myriad strangenesses. Some of them had been better than absent adults, the kind of people she could have stayed with if she'd been less acutely aware of how her ways weren't their ways, even if she had no concrete idea what her ways were yet. But that doesn't matter right now. She just wants Francis to talk.

"I think—I think Catherine came here because we've got—"

"Blood." It clicks, all of a sudden. Whatever Catherine wants to do, she must want to use their father's blood—or, better yet, bones. Jamie looks up at the ceiling and shivers. Nobody knows who they are, the anonymous dead of these caverns and crypts—but after all, magic can do all kinds of things thought to be impossible.

But what, she wonders, does Catherine need the bones for in the first place?

Jamie is lighting flames, old torches along the far wall coming to life with guttering reluctance as she presses her lighter to the pitch.

Francis catches his breath before he looks up and is met with a curving wall of bones, all pressed in together, skulls and spines and grinning mandibles with dirt between their teeth. He recoils, shaken to the core.

Jamie pauses, last torch flickering to life beneath her hand.

"What—" Francis is at a loss for words more often than he'd like, but in this moment, he can't force anything else out, confronted with the knowledge that this vast edifice of spent life must be what Catherine is looking for.

"This isn't on the byways," Jamie explains, coming to stand next to him as he pushes himself to his feet, reaching a hand out to lay a fingertip on the nearest forehead, the thrum of power almost electric as she makes contact. "Cross Bones. They tried to dig through this, people who had no idea what they were disturbing. For the trains, if you can believe it." She grins, teeth almost matching those of the remains she's touching, oblivious to the picture she makes, settling wholly into whatever communion she has with this place as Francis watches in morbid fascination.

"The way was blocked," a familiar voice intones from behind them. Francis jerks, startled out of his contemplation of how horrifying it must have been to encounter this when you weren't looking for it, or looking to disturb it; now he's facing a horror of a different kind, one partly of his own making.

Catherine tilts her head over to one side, looking sideways at them, as though the odd angle will reveal their secrets. Francis' hands start to shake, a strange, unsettling warmth rippling through his chest.

Jamie lets out a low gasp, sounding almost euphoric, though not exactly surprised. Her fingers are still resting in the bones as she looks over her shoulder, eyes slowly clearing. "You know how to make an entrance."

"I wouldn't have had to, if you'd been better at your job," Catherine says, "It took you long enough."

Jamie steps away from the wall, advancing slowly enough that Francis can almost believe she's still enthralled by whatever it is she finds so appealing about the bones. But he's attuned to her now, has spent time watching her, and he recognizes this from the second night, the easy measured stride, the faint smile on her lips.

"I used to hide in here too, you know," she says. "Don't know why I didn't think of it sooner, but then, it's hard to find." She stops in front of Catherine, looking steadily up at her despite their difference in height, Catherine's solid weight opposite Jamie's quick, narrow body.

Jamie's right that she'd be no good if it came to blows, but Francis doesn't think Catherine entirely knows who she's dealing with. He spurs himself to action, instead of just watching, watching, watching, and joins them, gathered under the highest part of the ceiling, firelight throwing moving shadows. "Catherine—"

"Going to call Mother down on me now, are you?" Catherine spits. "I won't let you do it."

"No," he retorts, and she actually looks a little surprised. "Why did you do all of this? If you wanted me to follow you all the way out here—down here—why bother with all of this—*bullshit*—"

Catherine just looks at him for a long moment, and then smiles. "Because if I hadn't," she says, "you would never have believed me."

Jamie's trying not to breathe too hard, trying to avoid drawing attention to herself. It's difficult. From just a meter away, she can't help but stare at the two of them: now that she isn't looking through Catherine's eyes but has her in front of her, she can finally see the resemblance between them. They're certainly twins, though nobody would be able to call them identical. It's less a case of physical parity and more that watching them standing beside each other, moving around the same room as though repelled by similar poles, Jamie has to fight off the dissonance of the overlap.

Francis looks startled at Catherine's words, surprise written on his face. Catherine, meanwhile, turns her gaze toward Jamie, pinning her where she stands. "You're not going to stop me?"

"I don't know what you're *doing*," Jamie says frankly. When she glances over at Francis she can see the fever flush in his cheeks, and feel the rush of his blood in duplicate, so strange and pronounced in its proximity.

Catherine looks between them, taller than Francis by a fraction. She's hollow under the eyes, almost as gaunt in the cheeks as Francis is becoming, and laughs, long throat exposed and vulnerable for one long moment before she looks back down. "Really? You chase me down and expect me to have all the answers when you find me? No more planning, no more digging on your own?" She goes quiet, fixing Francis with a stare Jamie doesn't like, as though she's taken his measure enough times to warrant her dismissal. "Well, at least I know you haven't changed."

Francis bristles, prickling through Jamie's awareness as a low heat, and she realizes this is what his anger feels like, the slow roil of it calm but pervasive, seeping into the cracks between them. "You're wrong," he whispers, voice a careful, brittle thing, but Catherine stiffens, narrowing her eyes. "I left."

Catherine's rigid expression shifts. "Really," she says. "I thought you were sent."

"I'm not here to take you back," he tells her. "If that's what you think."

She tilts her head to the side. "What are you here for then, Francis?"

His breathing is shallow, uneven. Jamie can feel it just like she can feel Catherine's anticipation. "I told you," he says.

"I need to know—what it is you're doing. What's going on. I need to know—"

"What you are," Jamie finishes, without meaning to: the words just slip out. She doesn't know whether she's speaking her own words or Francis'. But seeing them side-by-side like this, pieces are beginning to fall together. *What am I missing?* she wonders. It's like there's a puzzle piece that she's missing, that just won't fall into place.

Catherine glances over at her and smiles before turning back to Francis, eyes burning. "We're the same," she says simply, and Jamie's skin prickles.

"She needed a girl to carry the line," Catherine continues. "The others had all tried and tried and all gotten boys. And instead she got... us." She pauses while Francis looks on, confused, but Jamie almost knows what she's about to say before she says it.

"We were something in-between, not one or the other—someone in-between she'd never be able to control. I wish I could see what her face looked like when she first saw us. She must have been so horrified at her own failure. So she did what I guess must have seemed like a logical solution. She split us."

For a long moment it feels like none of them breathes. All the blood has drained from Francis' face. Jamie's brain is racing, trying to fit everything together. It all makes sense:

Francis' fatigue, his cousin's prophetical warnings, the blood—
the blood. Their blood is the same. She was right.

"Why—" Francis starts, voice hoarse. "Why would she—
why would anyone do that?" He knows, of course; he just
doesn't want to admit it. Jamie thinks on what it means, to
really want your own way badly enough that you'd split your
child in half. She thinks she knows what it must have taken
to do it, too, and the thought makes her shudder. She can only
imagine that the power must have been blinding—she must
have been drunk on it. Desperate.

Jamie wonders who had to die to give both of them
life, but she thinks she knows the answer to that question,
too.

"I don't believe you," Francis says, but he already sounds
doubtful, and Catherine knows: Jamie can tell. She has the
expression of a predator.

"There was always something wrong with us," she says.
"Couldn't you tell? Sometimes I wondered whether I was
even there. Like if I looked in the mirror there might not be
anything looking back. I know that doesn't make any sense—I
couldn't change like the rest of you could, so I should have
felt more solid. But it wasn't like that. You must have felt like
that too, right? Like you were a ghost."

Francis looks like he's about to be ill. "I don't know what
you're talking about," he says.

"And I hated it there," Catherine says, taking a step forward. Francis steps back. "I hated not being able to leave, I hated all their petty rivalries, I hated all those *boys*. I just wanted to be normal."

"We're not normal, Catherine," Francis says quietly, and she grins broadly.

"I know," she says. "Now I know. But it's different.

"I dug around in her desk when she was out doing her monthly patrol of the border," she continues. "I was trying to find information about Dad. They never talk about him, and I thought—that's weird, too. That seems *wrong*. I found some stuff. I found some information about his family—just enough that I could do my own research. Did you know his family lived in London for centuries? They're all dead now. They were one of the only clans of shifters who lived in one of the big cities in Europe. A lot of them are apparently buried here, in this very room." Francis starts at that, and she laughs. "Cross Bones. Some of their bones twisted, did you know that could happen? I saw it once. Inhuman bones. I can't see any here, so maybe the story's a lie. They weren't exactly making careful records. I feel like I can feel—*something*, though, can't you? Something in the air.

"But I found something even more interesting in our dear mother's desk," she says, pulling a piece of paper out of her back pocket and carefully unfolding it. Francis eyes it, leery, as though it might spontaneously catch fire. "I found a birth certificate.

Well, first I found both of ours. But then I found this one. Really buried. I'm surprised she didn't destroy it. Maybe she felt guilty. Maybe she knew this would happen one day and was just... leaving clues." She hands it over to him. "Take it. *Take it.* Look at it."

Francis takes it hesitantly, and looks down. He immediately frowns. Jamie's nerves are so on edge they're practically singing. "Who is this?" he asks, and Catherine laughs. It's not a particularly pleasant sound.

"That's *us*," she says, and Francis just stares down at it for a long moment longer before Catherine plucks it out of his hands and walks over to Jamie. "Care for a look?"

There's a photograph attached to the faded piece of paper of an infant with a scrunched face wrapped in a hospital blanket. The name is listed as *FRANCES* and there's no gender marked at all. "Is that allowed?" asks Jamie.

"Why would they have gone to a hospital at all?" Francis asks mulishly. "We don't ever—"

"Don't you remember," Catherine asks, eyes glowing. "The whole story. The birth was going terribly, and Dad freaked out, and took her—"

Francis blinks, something dawning on him. "And she was so mad..."

"Yes," Catherine said. "And if they hadn't there wouldn't ever have been a record. But there was, and she kept it.

I guess the clerk was sympathetic to our... situation. Or maybe they threatened her. Nobody can say no to Mother about anything, isn't that right?"

"How the hell do you know all of this?" Francis huffs, taking another step back. "So there's a birth certificate, so what? Maybe this baby died, maybe they forgot to put in an 'F', maybe—"

"Because," Catherine whispers, leaning close to him, "I got it all out of Amos before I left."

Francis stops moving.

"I got it out of Amos," Catherine says. "I told him what I thought and I asked him all my questions and he broke down and told me everything he knew. He was young but he wasn't too young to have forgotten everything."

"I don't believe you," Francis says, but it's weak.

"Do you know how she did it?" Catherine asks. Her voice is very low. Jamie feels a current of dread that could be hers or Francis'; she can't tell anymore. "Do you know how she made one baby two?"

"Stop," Francis says. "Stop talking."

"Maybe you do," Catherine says, turning to Jamie. "You're the blood worker."

Jamie swallows. "Someone would have to die."

"That's exactly right," Catherine says, smile wide and slightly unhinged. "Somebody had to die. And who do you think that was?" She turns back to Francis, who's looking past her, at something none of them can see.

"Stop talking," he says again.

"They made Amos watch," Catherine says. "They made all of them watch. What do you think that did to them?"

"Shut *up*," Francis says, and turns and vanishes back into the darkness of the tunnel.

Francis' heart is pounding. His body seems to have made an instant recovery now that Catherine is nearby again—he isn't having any trouble seeing in the dark—but that hardly seems to matter anymore. He can barely think, or maybe he's thinking too much. He tells himself that it's impossible, what she's told him—the idea that he isn't a person like other people are. Not whole in some way. He and Catherine have always been close—unsettlingly close—but...

But some small part of him is whispering: *What if she's right?* He thinks back to the way the cousins always treated them: as though they were less than human. The way that he always seemed to know exactly what Catherine was thinking. The hollowness inside of him that he never wanted to or knew how to acknowledge: the lack of curiosity. A slight sluggishness sometimes, the feeling that he could just sink back into the earth. He tries to imagine a person made up of both him and Catherine, and shudders. That person would be better, he thinks, than either of them. But he is himself. Isn't he?

He hears Jamie coming before he sees her, and hunches his shoulders. She appears in the mouth of the tunnel, chewing at her cuticles until they're bleeding: he can smell the blood. He waits for her to come closer before he speaks. "The rats are gone," he says, pointing at the canopy and trying to ignore the tremor in his voice. "Maybe we scared them off for good."

She frowns. He thinks she's annoyed. "At least I know why it was so hard to pin her down, now," she says, voice catching. "Can't even say it was my fault." She takes a deep breath. "So what does this make you?

He blinks, and considers her, to distract himself from thoughts of Catherine. It doesn't seem like they only met yesterday. Then, they'd just been two fractured people looking for a third. Now, he can admit that she's a something a little more to him than that. He's honestly surprised she's still here. She could have taken her money and run instead of leading him down into this mess—but here they are.

"I don't know," he says honestly. "I have no idea. Nothing."

She blanches. "I don't think that's exactly fair."

He lets out a low laugh. "Who knows," he says. "It's like—" he starts, and then stops. He doesn't know how to say it without sounding preposterous, overblown. *If she's telling the truth, my entire life has been a lie. I don't know who I am anymore. I don't know who I ever was.*

He swallows, and starts again. "I've lived at home... my whole life," he says slowly. "All I've ever done was because my mother told me to. Or Catherine told me to. Or my Uncle Gordon, or Marcus, or—" He shrugs. "Awful things, sometimes. Even if she's lying—or wrong—"

She tucks her hands into her pockets and doesn't say anything for a moment. "I used to do other things," she says, and then clarifies. "Other than this kind of blood magic. Than just finding people. I did—all kinds of things. Some of it was pretty... unpleasant. I never really thought about it while I was doing it. I was just... excited. By the challenge." She scuffs one of her feet against the floor. "I stopped after a while. I did some things I wish I hadn't. And now I'm here. And you're here," she says with a shrug. "Which isn't home."

He swallows, looking down at his hands, curled in his lap. "I—don't leave." His voice is weak, pathetic, but she just laughs, the sound raw, almost involuntary. It echoes, bouncing off the ceiling.

"I've come this far, haven't I? I couldn't leave even if I wanted to. I've got to see how this thing plays out. You think I'm just going to wonder for the rest of my life what happens to the two of you? You must be out of your mind.

"So," she continues. "What now?"

"I don't know. I don't know, but I don't—" His frustration builds, shoulders rising, long fingers curling into fists, pale in the darkness. "How could anyone tell?"

Jamie takes another step forward. "I just find people," she says. "Doesn't mean I know what makes them."

"Don't leave." Francis just looks at her, and can feel his face dragged crooked by more than just his expression. He shifts without thinking about it, when Catherine is nearby, and here he is again, caught halfway. "Please."

"All right," Jamie says, sitting down next to him, and neither of them says anything for a while, Jamie chewing on her cuticles.

Finally, she looks over at him. "You should go talk to her," she says. "I'll be here until you tell me to go."

Francis swallows. He manages a nod, and gets up, walking back to the other room.

Catherine has her back to the opening, the jagged sweep of her hair brushing her hunched shoulders dark in the flickering light of the sconces Jamie lit earlier. "Had a nice chat?" she says a little sourly, without turning around.

"What's the point of all this, Catherine?" he asks. He's still so, so tired. "Are you just going to drag me around with you for the rest of your life, if you don't want to go home?"

"What home is there to go to?" she asks, flexing her hand against the wall. "Everybody's dead or trying to kill each other."

Francis grinds his teeth. "Fine," he says. "But we can't be apart. If what you're saying is true."

She turns around, looking at him incredulously. "Do you really not believe me? Do you want to know why I left, Francis? I left because I knew that if I tried to tell you at home that you'd think I was crazy. But I thought that if I came all the way out here—if you *felt* it—if you felt what it *did*—"

He stares at her. "Were you that sure?" he asks. He's never really been able to imagine it, the kind of steely confidence Catherine has always seemed to have, though now he wonders if she wasn't always trying to compensate for something. For some emptiness inside of herself that she could never fill.

She blinks. "No," she says, and he thinks he might have surprised it out of her. "I was proving it to myself, too."

"So, what," he says wearily. "We move somewhere, live in the same apartment forever—"

There's a strange light in her eyes. "Haven't you figured it out?" she asks. "I'm going to put us back together."

For a moment he doesn't understand what she even means—and then it hits him. He takes a step back, reeling as though struck. "You're crazy," he says. "You're crazy, Catherine, you—"

"No," she said, "it was crazy for them to do it. *She* was crazy. Do you really want to live like this forever, Francis? Like we have been living? These—half-lives?"

"I want to live *my* life," Francis replies, although he's not entirely sure what that means.

"You don't have a life," Catherine says harshly. "Neither of us does."

"Don't say that," he says. "Don't say that, we—"

"We're not *real*," she says desperately.

"Even if what you're saying is true," he says, "that doesn't mean—that wouldn't mean—you're *real*, Catherine. I'm *real*."

"Amos told me how she did it," she says, voice low. "They were all in the woods and she led Dad out there without telling him what she was doing. He figured out that something was wrong but by then it was too late. Nobody dreamed of questioning her authority back then. You know her. She's terrifying. She apologized and they held him back while she slit his throat. And then we were born. So I guess you could say he gave birth to us as much as she did.

"All of these bones in this room," she whispers. There's a faint echo. "Piled above us. His family's bones. That's power. And we have her—this blood worker friend of yours. We can *do* it."

"Can she just—do that?" he asks dubiously. "If somebody died to make it happen—"

"I've done research," she said. He's realized what she looks like: she looks feverish. He wonders if maybe they are living some kind of half-lives, like this: if they're both just burning up, racing toward their expiration dates. "There aren't exactly a lot of clear-cut manuals, but to bring somebody back to life, somebody has to die—but we're both alive—and just need to go back to what we were originally—"

It seems close enough to the same thing to Francis, and besides, he's not ready to agree. It would be like jumping off a cliff and trusting that you'd wake up in another body— with a different mind. Or like having enough faith in a particular kind of reincarnation to hold a gun to your head and pull the trigger. He isn't quite sure that he has that kind of confidence.

He turns and sees Jamie lingering in the entranceway. Catherine turns to look, too, when she sees his glance. "There you are," she says. "You're going to put us back together."

"No, I'm not," Jamie says frankly.

"Oh yes," says Catherine, "I think you are."

"I'm not going to kill anybody," Jamie says flatly, "so no, sorry. I'm not. And don't threaten to use me as your human sacrifice, or whatever; I can't do the magic and use *myself.*"

"You don't need to," Catherine says. "Nobody's being born—"

"*If* I were going to do this," Jamie says, voice flat, "and *if* you're even telling the truth, and not just out of your mind, someone would definitely be born. Neither of you is this—other person.

You could even say that person died at some point and is being resurrected, which only further emphasizes my point."

For a moment, Catherine looks lost, and Francis feels almost bad for her. Then, her eyes gleam, and she says: "What if you killed one of *us*?"

Jamie blanches. "I don't exactly know that that would work, either," she says. "Since I'd be trying to—splice the two of you, or whatever exactly it is. If one of you died—"

"What would happen to the other one?" Francis finishes.

"Right," Jamie says. "To do something like this, you need a—ugh, *sacrifice*, a blood worker, and something to boost it, like this place. But you need all of them."

Catherine looks around, desperate. "But—but—there has to be a way," she says. "I planned—I planned it all out. I—"

"It really doesn't seem like you planned much of anything," says Jamie sharply.

Francis thinks about telling her: *I never agreed in the first place.* But it seems useless. She's already lost. They could go up to the street, find someone, bring them back down here—but they're not going to kill anybody. And part of him still doesn't entirely believe her, despite the fact that nothing she's said is impossible. He's lived, after all, an entire life. To believe that he shouldn't have is something he can't quite face yet. The irony isn't lost on him that it's only now that he's built up an entire set of memories that he doesn't share with Catherine: now, just as she's trying to tell him that they're one and the same.

Catherine is standing in the middle of the room, looking between the two of them, light flickering around the walls. She looks small somehow, despite the fact that she's slightly taller than he is. "I *will* do it," she says, voice uncharacteristically shrill. "I *will*—"

"Such determination, daughter. I admire your dedication, though I can't say I endorse your methods."

Francis freezes as though paralyzed for a second time since going underground. Catherine has gone stock still in front of him. Out of the corner of his eye, he sees Jamie turn, eyes widening slightly.

"Mother," Catherine says, sounding strangled. "What a surprise."

❦

Jamie wonders for a fleeting, desperate moment whether she could just melt into the walls. There's enough latent energy here—could she, perhaps, work up a good enough glamour to simply vanish, and slink out of the room invisibly? Her determination to stay seems to melt away in the face of this woman: so identifiably an older version of Francis and Catherine, but with a greater, more terrifying force behind her.

Now that she's in front of them, Jamie's amazed she didn't feel her coming. Maybe she was disguising herself. She feels more powerful than anybody Jamie's ever met, except maybe Jack.

She's still vaguely contemplating potential escape routes when the woman turns her gaze straight toward her, and the hairs on the back of her neck stand straight up. She looks like Francis, but she doesn't have his clear eyes: hers are dark, bottomless. "So you're the little fly that's been hanging around my Francis," she says, eyes gleaming. "Not exactly what I was expecting."

Jamie swallows. "What were you expecting?"

The woman smiles. "I suppose I'm not sure," she says. "Francis hasn't ever spent much time associating with strangers."

"Can't imagine why that might be," Jamie replies.

"How did you find us?" Catherine croaks.

"Don't be silly, darling," their mother replies. "You're my children. I always know where you are."

"Your *child*, you mean," Catherine snarls. "Isn't that right?"

"I have no idea what you mean," she replies blithely. "Don't leave out poor Francis, now. He's had enough of that already."

Catherine lets out an incredulous little laugh. "And you want to blame that on *me*?"

Her mother levels her gaze at her. Jamie practically shudders, imagining it secondhand. She glances over at

Francis: his expression is shuttered. He hasn't moved since she appeared.

"Maybe you've forgotten," she says. "I used to call you aside, to train you—to teach you what I knew. To prepare you. Of course there were all kinds of things you didn't take to. You've never had my power, my dear. I hate to say it, but it's only the truth. But still—you remember everything I taught you. How much I tried to groom you. Yes?

"But you used to *gloat*, Catherine, when Francis wanted to come too," she continues. "Of course that was impossible. That's not how it works. Some secrets can't be passed along to just anyone. And the family falls apart without its leader. The clan dies. So poor Francis couldn't get your education." Francis' shoulders have hunched. "And you liked being the special one. You liked being my favorite. Didn't you?" Catherine is shaking her head, but her face tells a different story. "Yes. You used to taunt him and push him out of the room, you used to make him miserable. And you enjoyed it.

"I'm willing to forgive you and bring you both home," she says. "But this silliness must stop."

"You did it," Catherine says, voice shaking. "I have—I have the document. Amos told me. He's *dead* now," she adds, voice shaking. "They're all dead. Is Uncle Gordon going to show up, too? We might as well get rid of the whole family in one go, while we're at it."

Their mother considers her for a moment; Jamie can practically see the gears turning in her mind. "You know that disputes over succession are a part and parcel of being part of a clan," she says calmly. "Some amount of bloodshed is inevitable. If your cousins were foolish enough to listen to Gordon's suggestions, then there's not much I could have done for them." When Catherine starts to make an incredulous noise, she continues, "And so what if I did? This is what you want, isn't it? A confession. But you've been different people your entire lives. You were the only one in the room with me, Catherine. Don't think I've forgotten how often you used to fight. The awful things you used to do to each other. You can't erase that with some little spell. You can't *fix* it."

Catherine looks up at her. "I can try," she says. "At least I have the—the *choice*—"

"*You* do? I thought that took two," their mother replies, sounding amused. "Or has Francis agreed to your little scheme?" She doesn't say anything. "Have you, Francis?"

Francis' throat works. His jaw is locked together and there are muscles straining in his neck. "See?" their mother says, turning back to Catherine. "You've hardly worked this out, darling, but it's no tragedy, you're still very young, and unpracticed. You need me, I'd say—"

Jamie still has an eye on Francis, so she almost misses Catherine lashing out, one arm extended, hand twisted, clawed.

She hears her low, guttural cry as clear as anything, though. By the time she's turned to look, the space where their mother was standing has been replaced by an enormous bear, which opens its mouth and roars, pushing itself up over Catherine.

Jamie stumbles backward, scrambling to feel for the wall, and almost gets bowled over by the creature that was (and is) Francis, hurling himself at his mother. The two of them topple over: he's smaller, but fiercer, and manages to propel her across the room and away from his sister, who's lying, shaking, on the ground, looking as fully human as Jamie does on any given day.

Jamie glances over at the exit. It's just close enough to Francis and his mother that the thought of passing through it is less than appealing, and far enough away that it seems doable. She stands tottering on the brink of a decision, glancing at Catherine, who's still lying, shaking on the ground, as though she's in shock—which, Jamie figures, she probably is.

She looks back over at Francis, whose mother has just walloped his head to the side. They're both smearing blood across the ground. Something begins to click in her mind, one link following the next.

She drops to the ground and crawls over to Catherine, wrapping her fingers around her leg and pulling her back over to the wall, watching the blurred bodies across the room as she does so. They don't seem to notice. Catherine makes a brief noise of protest before having the good sense to shut up, and then just looks at her in confusion.

"You're sure you want to do the spell?" Jamie whispers. Catherine stares at her blankly for a moment, and then nods. "I won't do it unless Francis says it's all right. But if he does— then I think I can. All right?"

"Okay," Catherine says, confused.

"She's not going to kill either of you," Jamie says, impatient. "She's just trying to scare you. She can't kill you, and she doesn't know what'll happen if she kills him. And you need to kill someone to do the magic."

Catherine's eyes go wide. Jamie's surprised she hadn't worked it out earlier, though it had taken her longer than it should have, too. It's hard to imagine killing her: that woman. But everyone dies sometime.

"How?" Catherine asks.

Jamie looks up at the bones. "Your mother's very powerful," she says. "Fortunately, I have an advantage."

London is hers in a way it isn't theirs. She's a part of the city by both nature and nurture, on intimate terms with its underbelly and its moments of fleeting beauty, immune to its chaos and dependent on it to amplify her, bolster her on cold nights and thin winters. She doesn't think Catherine really knew what she was doing when she brought them here, to this place of the longest and most unquiet dead. But Jamie does.

This woman and Jack are the most powerful people Jamie's ever met—but there's a reason Jack was so eager to keep Jamie in her thrall. And now she's got Francis and Catherine's blood running in her veins.

"Can I get a claw?" she whispers, just as the woman across the room seems to notice something is wrong. "Prick my finger, just there. I'm used to it, don't worry." The blood beads at her fingertip and she feels a deep, settled sense of satisfaction. This is what she's meant to be doing. She cracks her neck, shakes out her shoulders, and then rubs it between her thumb and forefinger before holding them up to the nearest flame. When they start to burn she smiles, and blows.

The fire races around the edge of the room. It's been so long since she did this kind of magic. Nobody ever wanted to hire her for this: it isn't the kind of thing you could outsource. You have to maintain it all the time, like Jack does at The Stag.

Francis and his mother leap away from the wall. Jamie licks her lips and lets the magic settle in her, and then starts to pull on all of the dead around them, all the nameless souls that history forgot, some of whom have finally ended in the people standing in front of her—until each one is a thread wrapped around her hand.

By the time she's done, they're all huddled in the middle of the room, looking like humans. "What," growls their mother from where she's sitting on the floor, "have you done."

"We're on neutral ground now," Jamie says, almost giddy. Francis' eyes grow wide. "You may find your abilities—impaired."

She scoffs. "Neutral ground doesn't hold me, my dear. It's very sweet of you to—"

"Go ahead," Jamie croaks, smiling. "Try."

And she does. Her skin ripples. Her face elongates into something almost dog-like. She can draw claws. Her teeth grow sharp. But she can't do what she was doing only moments ago. Jamie silently thanks Catherine and Francis' blood for the extra hold she has on all of them, thrumming under her skin.

Their mother looks murderous. "I will kill you with my own two hands—" she begins, but Catherine hastily steps in front of her.

"I wouldn't do that, Mother," she says, trying to contain her glee. "That would be foolish."

Her mother looks up at her, expression savage. "How dare you," she says, voice low and rough. "How dare you tell me what I can and can't do. If it weren't for me, you wouldn't exist. Neither of you would exist. You would be one—unnatural creature. I gave birth to you twice, and here you are, defying me. I should have cast you out. So many miscarriages and then—you. You were a—a *disappointment*," she spits out. "From the first moment you were alive. Now I have two of you. Two miserable disappointments."

"You're not making a great case for yourself, Mother," Catherine says.

She breathes heavily. "You really want to be put back together?" she says. "I can do it. I know the spell. You need blood for that. Kill that girl. Who is she? Nobody. Gordon's destroyed the clan—we can try to rebuild it. Find some other shifters. I'm your *mother*, for god's sake."

"So we should kill her, and trust you?" Francis says quietly.

She turns very slowly to stare at him. Neither of them says anything for a long, long moment.

"Francis," Jamie says. "What do you want to do?"

He's still looking down at his mother. "Do it," he says. "Do it."

He has to practically leap back to avoid her, but soon enough has her arms behind her back. "Catherine?" he pants. "Give me a hand?"

She hurries over to grab one of their mother's arms. She's shouting nonsense, but Jamie isn't listening, and she doesn't think Francis or Catherine is, either. There's magic vibrating in the air and in her bones.

"Are you sure?" she asks Francis, and he looks her straight in the eye, steady, and nods. She swallows.

"I need you to draw some of your own blood," she says. "Each of you. Or each other's, it doesn't really matter."

Francis works one of his arms free and reaches over to slice open Catherine's cheek. She's got an almost ecstatic expression on her face as she turns to do the same. Jamie would have expected fingers, but she won't complain. She awkwardly reaches out to smear her hand against both their cheeks and clenches it and unclenches it. Their blood is still fizzing in her veins. "Could you nick me again?" she asks Catherine, holding out her palm, and when all of their blood mixes together she feels electric: this is the feeling she's been missing. Like she could do anything.

Magic feels almost physical sometimes. Some people, who do other kinds, recite words or chants. Jamie feels the humming currents of the earth and weaves them and splits them apart. She pulls everything as close together as it can be before the last push, and then crouches down in front of the woman who gave birth to some version of the people standing behind her: her face can't hold steady, shifting rapidly between features, quick enough to induce nausea. "You're going to die," Jamie says, almost kindly. She does feel like a kind of god. She'll come down from this later. It won't be pretty. It never is.

"Say your goodbyes now," she says to Catherine and Francis, but they just look at each other and shake their heads. "All right. Who's doing the deed? I don't have a knife on me."

"You do it," Catherine says, and Francis says, "All right," and there are a few seconds where their mother lets out a wild sound before he slices her artery open, and it bursts forth.

Jamie puts her hand in the blood. It's warm. Fresh. Four of them are mixed together on her hand now. She can feel it starting. Stinging. Singing. She closes her eyes and brings her palm to her nose and smells it: it smells good, better than anything else on the earth. Nobody else will ever understand that, probably, except the others of her kind. She licks a stripe off the center, and shudders as she feels everything she pulled together start to rush into place. She licks again, and *twists*.

Live in a body for a certain period of time—

Life is a body sustained for a certain amount of time. The finite body is a fact of life most people take at a base value: a person is born; a person lives; the body expires. That spark, that light, that innate thing that *animates*—that's something else.

If Francis' body is many bodies, rushing into each other and over each other... is the thing inside him that animates many things? Is it fluid, changeable but the same, expanding to fill its container? Is it the flesh itself that provides the spark? He hasn't ever wondered. He's always just shifted. He is a creature of instinct.

This must be what it feels like to die slowly, he thinks, this gradual loss of space—first hands, feet, arms, legs, heart, and lungs— and then, finally, the windows close, and the spark goes out.

Or, worse, the thing inside screams for a while, batters at its cage, and then finally succumbs.

Francis curls his fingers in towards his palms, smallest first, thumb folding down over the top, and *wills*, as hard as he has ever tried—

There. A flicker. A rift in the armor, or just a last-gasp reflex obeying him as it fades, leaving behind only a fist, long blunt fingers and a long blunt thumb curled into a broad palm.

Live in a body for a certain amount of time, and you get used to it.

Live in a body for a certain amount of time—

His body is only a body in half. Something pulls at him, but it's familiar. It's safe. He lets himself be pulled. It's easy, in the end, to let go.

❧

Jamie stares up at the ceiling, startled out of whatever trance she was in, blood still rushing in her ears. It's started to shake: she can feel the vibrations all the way down into her bones. They're going to come loose soon, she realizes, all those bones. They're going to fall.

She turns to look down: she's covered with arterial blood up to the elbows, and her clothes aren't much better. It looks like she's killed someone, which in a way, she definitely has.

Next to the dead body is—whoever the person who used to be Francis and Catherine is, sprawled over the ground, unconscious, just as bloody. It's a more slender body, a little taller. Jamie thinks she can see some of Francis' and some of Catherine's features in the face. Her skin prickles, as she looks. She can't decide whether the effect is incredibly unnatural or somehow exactly—right. But it doesn't much matter at the moment, because if they don't leave right now, none of this is going to matter: they'll be dead in a matter of minutes.

"Get up!" she shouts, and they—she guesses they're a they—blink, discombobulated. Something in the ceiling cracks. "We're about to get buried alive, time to get moving!"

They blink again, and look down, first frowning and then widening their eyes, incredulous.

"Come *on!*" Jamie shouts, grabs their arm, and drags them toward the opening, just as the bones begin to fall, first a few, then more, a slow ripple going back hundreds of years, hundreds of meters, hundreds of thousands of seconds of lives breathed out as they clatter and crash to the ground behind them, pushing them on and on and on. The person who was once Francis and Catherine is clumsy at first, awkward in their new body, and as they're forced to hurtle forward, they slowly come back to themselves: she can see it out of the corner of her eye, how each step lands more firmly, breath coming in long pulls instead of gasps, lungs and heart and limbs resolving into a whole.

They finally spill out at the riverfront, panting. Jamie can't help thinking about what the gatekeeper will think about the fact that Cross Bones is gone. Everyone who uses these places will be furious, most likely. It feels like some kind of blank space in her mind: a gap. It's probably better this way, though, she thinks. Dark things have happened down there.

The sky is gray: it looks like it's about to rain. She blinks, disoriented. It feels like she's been underground for days, but she knows she hasn't—she's not sure how long it's been, all told. She looks down at the blood on her clothes. It looks less bright in the dim daylight. She'll probably have to try to work some kind of glamour to get home without getting arrested.

Finally she looks over at the person standing next to her. They're looking up at the sky, squinting slightly, eerily still.

"You all right?" she asks, and they turn to look at her. She recognizes the same wide, pale eyes she's come to find familiar set in a slightly unfamiliar face, and tries not to find it too disorienting. She thinks those eyes might be brighter than she remembers, as though the glassiness Jamie associated with Francis at his most exhausted state has receded like a breaking fever—but then, that may just be the daylight. There's a long pink scar down their cheek, recently healed. She looks down at her palm: the sliced cut there is healed, too.

"I think so," they say. She doesn't recognize the voice—except that she does. It's two tones resolved into some melodious note in the middle.

"Well, good," she says, rubbing at her temples. She has a killer headache coming on, the inevitable result of this kind of work. The comedown was quick this time.

She looks over again: they're looking at their hands, now. Francis had big hands. These are smaller, more graceful, but the fingers are still long, tapering. Jamie can't imagine it, the idea of waking up in a new body, but the other part—waking up with a new mind, or part of one—is even stranger.

"What's it like?" she asks, although she's not sure if she should.

"Different," they reply after a moment. "Sort of." They frown. "It's like—trying to breathe with one lung. And then having two. But you're still breathing either way."

"I think I know what you mean," Jamie says.

"What are you doing to call yourself?" she asks after a moment's pause. They seem to consider this, thoughtful.

"I don't know. What do you think?" they ask, turning to her, and she lets out a startled little laugh.

"Don't ask me," she says. "I don't think I should be the one to tell you. Doesn't seem right, does it?"

"I don't know," they say. "Seems better than her. I don't think she really liked me much."

"No," Jamie agrees. "I didn't exactly get that impression."

"Sorry to have made you—you know," they say.

"I didn't do anything," Jamie says mildly. "That was all you, in case you've forgotten." She feels curiously unbothered by it—maybe it'll catch up with her later. All she can bring herself to feel right now is a kind of bone-deep exhaustion, and a low, suppressed ache that she's trying not to think about.

They don't say anything for a while, just watch the river. Birds are flying overhead, cawing sharply. "Can you do that?" Jamie asks, apropos of nothing.

"What?" they ask.

"You know," Jamie says. "That. Do birds. Fly."

"Oh," they say. "Yes. Not very often."

"That's what I'd want to do," Jamie says. "If I were, you know. One of you people."

They smile a little. It's reminiscent of Catherine. "Yes," they say. "You people."

"Sorry," Jamie says. "You know what I mean."

"Yes," they say. "Maybe I'll try it more often now. And then, a moment later: "You miss him?"

"What?" Jamie says. "No." A couple of days is nothing, really, in the grand scheme of things, and her life has been full of incident. But she can't deny that this feels like a particularly significant couple of days, can't deny that when she cleans off the blood she's been washed in, she'll feel something slightly different than she normally would have, back when she did things like this more often. Though of course, she's never really done anything "like this" before.

"I never miss anyone."

"Sure," they say, sounding amused, and Jamie looks away, embarrassed. She isn't prone to feeling much sympathy for people. She sees so many people histrionic about cheating spouses, pathetically desperate to talk to family members they haven't seen in years. But for whatever reason she has found herself open here, with these people, some part of her raw and too exposed. Maybe she's just tired. Soon she'll be heading back to Sarit's, and her little temporary bed. Soon she'll get to sleep again, and this Francis-and-Catherine person will go… somewhere else.

The blood, she realizes, that has been rushing through her veins has vanished: burned up, probably; burned out. She's only herself again. They're themselves, too. It's a strangely liberating kind of isolation.

She takes a cigarette out with her bloody fingers. "You want one?" she asks, and they look at with the same almost bemused expression.

"All right," they say, and take it, twisting it in their fingers.

She lights hers, holding it to her lips and inhaling, and offers them a light, but they shake their head.

"That's for smoking, you know," Jamie says.

"Doesn't have to be," they say mildly. "Maybe I just want to keep it."

"Sure," Jamie says. "What are you going to do now? Go home, take over, new world order, that sort of thing?"

"Why, you interested?"

Jamie laughs. "No," she says. She doesn't think she could survive outside of London, if she's being honest. She's a city creature. Even the dirt and grit and grime here are her own.

The clouds are starting to clear, and the sunlight shines thinly down on the Thames. It's still early, she thinks. There's only a faint breeze and the smoke is hitting her lungs just right. She lets smoke stream out of her nostrils for the pleasure of it, the heat of it warming her from the inside. It's a beautiful morning.

"Well, you'd better light it," they say, holding out the cigarette, and Jamie can't help smiling a little, reaching out to flick her lighter. She wishes she still had enough fire in her to do it with her fingertips.

The flame licks up into the paper as the tobacco catches, and they smoke in companionable silence for a while, breathing the same tainted air, before Jamie stubs hers out and tosses it onto the silt and gravel. "You should pick a good name," she says. "Not many people get to choose."

"You could, if you wanted," they point out, though Jamie knows that's not really true: of course she *could*, but she is who she is. She's Jamie. They're going to have to figure that out for themselves.

They pitch the half-smoked cigarette into the water. "Ask me later," they say, eyes gleaming. "Maybe I'll tell you." And with that, they start to walk away, only barely brushing against Jamie's shoulder as they climb back to higher ground.

Jamie watches them leave until she can't see them anymore, and then turns back to the river. The sky clouds over again, and the birds keep circling and cawing. She lights another cigarette and smokes it down without moving, and then when she's finished, finally starts to make her wending way back to city level, hoping her glamour will hold. They're always shit, but she's feeling lucky. She thinks she'll go back to The Stag. Jack still owes her a few explanations, and she could use a drink, or four.

She breathes in the city when she steps onto the street—the foul smell of it, rubbish and petrol and magic—and smiles before vanishing into its endless, impenetrable maze.

Acknowledgements

Thank you to everyone who made this a reality, including but not limited to: everyone who backed us on KS, your faith I hope was not misplaced, and a special thank you to Deborah, without whom this would not exist. I would also like to thank everyone who lent a hand in editing, and Megan for the wonderful art.

About the Author

Natalie Wilkinson technically lives in the Thames, as her boat extends two feet below the water line. Having embraced the swamp witch aesthetic, her next book is about lesbian spies in space. Her hobbies include dressing like a Bond villain, avoiding her phone and heckling swans. She does not have any cats.

@causingfevers

www.ingramcontent.com/pod-product-compliance
Lightning Source LLC
Chambersburg PA
CBHW021020120726
47905CB00009B/3103